Against all Hope

Amanda Wills

ISBN: 1511615567
ISBN-13: 978-1511615563

In memory of Hamilton, my beautiful Connemara pony.
He was one in a million.

CHAPTER 1

Poppy McKeever held her breath and waited for the vet to speak. A dark cloud had followed her like a shadow all day. The suspense of not knowing was almost unbearable. Cloud's ears flicked anxiously back and forth and when Poppy looked down at her hands she realised she'd been clasping his leadrope so tightly that her knuckles had turned completely white. The vet lowered Cloud's leg to the ground and straightened her back. Poppy tried to read her expression but she was giving no clues. Her face was calm, composed, professional. In contrast, Poppy felt like screaming. Cloud's ribs jutted out like the furrows of a newly-ploughed field and his brown eyes were fixed on Chester. The donkey was watching the proceedings with interest from over the stable door while Poppy's brother, Charlie, was surreptitiously trying to listen to his own heartbeat with the vet's stethoscope. Her stepmother, Caroline, gave Poppy an encouraging smile, although she looked as pale and worried as Poppy did.

"Well," said the vet, her tanned arms reaching for her medicine bag. "Do you want the good news or the bad news?"

Poppy's heart sank. "The good news?"

"For a pony that's spent the last five years living wild on the moor he's in remarkably good shape. He is underweight and his teeth definitely need a rasp, but his eyes look healthy and his chest is as clear as a bell. There's nothing wrong with his general health, at least nothing that a bit of TLC won't sort out."

Poppy gave Caroline a quick smile. "But what about his leg?"

"Ah, that's the bad news, I'm afraid. As you know he's very lame on his near hind leg and we need to work out what's causing it. If it was a stone or an abscess in his foot or, say, a pulled tendon, it would be easy to spot. But I can't see or feel any obvious sign of injury." The vet ran her hand along Cloud's leg from his hock to his hoof again, shaking her head. "I think we'll have to get him to Tavistock and X-ray his foot. It may be a fractured pedal bone, which is a worry."

"What's a pedal bone and why is it worried?" asked Charlie, who had dropped the stethoscope on the ground and was making a beeline for the vet's bag of instruments, some of which looked as if they belonged in a medieval torture chamber. Caroline deftly swept the stethoscope and the bag off the ground and into the hands of the vet, who took them with a grateful smile.

"A pedal bone is a bone in a horse's foot," she told the three McKeevers. "It runs roughly from here to here." She drew a line with her index finger from the top to the bottom of Cloud's hoof. "Occasionally a horse can fracture its pedal bone. It's an impact injury. You could fracture it by landing heavily on a rock for example, which this chap could easily have done while he was out on the moor." She gave Cloud's bony rump a gentle pat and he shifted his weight to the other leg. "The only way to tell is with an X-ray. We'll get that done and hopefully we can rule it out."

"What happens if his pedal bone is fractured?" Poppy asked, her nails digging into the lead rope.

"Well, he would need to be fitted with a special shoe that immobilised his foot. A good farrier would be able to make that."

"My friend Ed's dad is a farrier!" said Charlie.

"There you are then. And once the shoe was fitted Cloud would need complete stable rest for up to two months. We'd X-ray his foot again after a few weeks to see if there were any signs of the bone healing and then it's a waiting game I'm afraid. If it does heal he should make a full recovery but if it doesn't it's not good news. He'll never be completely sound."

"You mean Poppy would never be able to ride him?" Caroline asked.

"No, I'm afraid not. Anyway, I'd better get going.

I've two more calls to make before evening surgery. Phone in the morning to make an appointment for the X-ray and once that's done we can see where we stand. In the meantime keep him in his stable, just to be on the safe side." The vet saw the lines crinkling Poppy's forehead. "It's no use worrying about something that might not happen. You concentrate on fattening him up and leave his foot to me."

Poppy nodded, her face a picture of gloom. She led Cloud into his stable while Caroline walked around the side of the house with the vet and watched as her mud-splattered Land Rover disappeared down the Riverdale drive. Chester whickered softly and gave the pony a nudge. Poppy slipped off his headcollar and gave them each a bucket of nuts.

The trauma of being rounded up in the annual drift and then sold at auction with the native Dartmoor ponies had taken its toll on Cloud. He'd been so exhausted the night before that he'd barely been able to stand up. As well as being as thin as a stick he shrank to the back of the stable if anyone except Poppy, Charlie or Caroline went near him. Poppy hoped his anxiety was something she could heal with time. But if his foot was broken would she even get the chance?

CHAPTER 2

"There you are!" said a familiar voice. Poppy turned to see her best friend Scarlett's freckled face, framed by dark red hair, peering into the stable. "Did Cloud have a good night? He's scoffing those nuts like there's no tomorrow but he still looks like an equine coat hanger, Poppy. I thought I heard a car on the drive. Was it the vet?"

Scarlett's chatter always cheered Poppy up and she felt more positive as she filled her friend in on the prognosis as they walked together into the kitchen.

Her dad was reading the paper at the kitchen table, his glasses perched on the end of his nose. Mike McKeever was a war correspondent for the BBC and when he wasn't on an assignment in one of the world's trouble spots he was based in London. It was unusual to find him at home. He smiled when he saw the girls.

"Hello Scarlett. How are your mum and dad?"

"Good thanks, though it's a busy time of year for them, what with the harvest and everything."

Caroline was chopping tomatoes. "Have you eaten?" she asked Scarlett, who shook her head. "Fancy some dinner? It's only pizza and salad."

"Sounds good to me," said Scarlett, sitting down. "Hey, have you heard the news?" The McKeevers looked at her blankly. "You know those two old cottages on the edge of the Blackstone farm? Jimmy Flynn, George Blackstone's farm hand, lives in one with his mum and dad but the other one's been empty since old Mrs Deakins died three years ago. Anyway, Mum says new people are moving in next week. And guess where they're coming from?"

"Crikey, I've no idea," said Caroline.

"London!" she announced. "You might even know them."

"Hardly likely, Scarlett. London is massive. Millions of people live there. It's not like Waterby where everyone's related," laughed Poppy.

Scarlett waved her hands airily. "Whatever. Anyway, it's a mum and her daughter, according to Jimmy's auntie's brother-in-law, who's married to one of my dad's second cousins."

"See what I mean?" said Poppy, raising her eyebrows at her dad and Caroline.

"I'm not sure how old the girl is and I have no idea what's happened to her dad," continued Scarlett. "One thing I do know - the cottage is an absolute dump. I wouldn't move there if you paid me. I went inside once with Mum not long before Mrs Deakins was taken into hospital. She was a nice old dear, although sadly lacking in the dental department."

"What?" asked Poppy's dad.

"She didn't have any teeth," Scarlett grinned.

"You are funny Scar. People moved in and out of our old street in Twickenham all the time. It's not that big news," Poppy said. But despite this her curiosity was stirred. It wasn't that long ago that the McKeevers had made the move from Twickenham to Devon in search of a quieter life.

"Once they're in we'll go and say hello," suggested Scarlett. Poppy wasn't keen on meeting new people but Waterby was such a small village she had to concede that this was a major event.

"If we must," she agreed reluctantly.

Cloud's X-ray was booked for the following Saturday. The week flew by. Poppy set her alarm for six every morning so she could spend an extra hour grooming the pony before school. She became familiar with the contours of his body and discovered that he loved being rubbed behind his ears but was ticklish under his stomach and stamped a back foot to remind her if she happened to forget. He leant on her when she picked up his feet and nibbled on his leadrope when he was bored. Poppy would sing her favourite hits to him as she trimmed his tail and combed his mane and she always went straight to his stable after school to spend another hour with him.

"He knows when you're on your way home," Caroline told her over dinner one night. "He starts banging on the stable door about ten minutes before the bus gets in. Anyone would think he's psychic."

When the time came to take Cloud to the veterinary surgery in Tavistock Caroline enlisted the help of Scarlett's dad Bill. He arrived at Riverdale with his Land Rover and trailer and they loaded first Chester and then Cloud. Poppy had been adamant that Chester should come too – she knew he would have a calming influence on the Connemara. Poppy spent the journey craning her neck to watch Cloud and Chester through the open slats of the trailer. The minute Bill pulled into the yard behind the surgery she unclicked her seatbelt and scrambled out. Cloud was damp with sweat and his ears jerked back and forth. She could feel him trembling beneath her touch. Chester, on the other hand, looked completely at ease.

Charlie led the old donkey down the ramp and Poppy followed with Cloud close behind. The vet appeared from the open doors of a building at the far end of the yard. "Follow me," she said. "The X-ray equipment is in the barn. We're all set up and ready to go. It shouldn't take too long."

The concrete yard was flanked on one side by a line of kennels under a wide pitched roof. Each kennel housed a different dog. Some lay quietly, sleeping off the anaesthetic from earlier operations, others whined or barked as Poppy and Charlie led Cloud and Chester past.

"These are the dogs that are in for treatment. The cats are all inside. We also have a couple of stables, but they're empty today," said the vet.

As Poppy turned to look at the stables Cloud stopped, raised his grey head and whinnied. She tugged his leadrope and clicked her tongue encouragingly. "Come on, Cloud. It's just an X-ray to see what's wrong with your leg. No-one's going to hurt you, I promise."

Chester's hairy rump was disappearing into the barn but Cloud refused to budge. He was staring at the last kennel before the double barn door, with feet planted firmly to the spot.

"What are you looking at, Cloud?" Poppy followed his gaze but all she could see was an empty kennel with what looked like a long-forgotten black and tan blanket crumpled in a heap in the corner. But as she stared the blanket stirred and a black head with a tan muzzle appeared. Cloud gave a whicker and the dog barked softly in response, its plumy tail thumping the ground.

"Oh! I thought it was an old blanket but it's a dog," she said to Caroline, who had joined her by the cage.

The dog was emaciated and its shaggy hair was matted in places. It struggled to its haunches and offered them its paw, which was swaddled in a cast and bandage, as if to shake hands.

"What happened to her?" Poppy asked.

"She's a he, actually," said the vet. "The police brought him in yesterday. He was found dodging the traffic on the Okehampton road. His leg was broken so I think he'd probably been hit by a car, though he was lucky – there's no damage internally."

"Who does he belong to?"

"I expect he was probably dumped. People do it all the time, I'm afraid. He'll stay with us for a few more days and then I'll ask Moorwings, the local animal sanctuary, to come and pick him up. They'll look after him until someone gives him a permanent home."

Charlie joined them, with Chester following patiently behind. Charlie leant his forehead against the wire cage to get a closer look at the dog, which seemed bemused by all the attention. "What's his name?"

"One of the veterinary nurses christened him Freddie after her first boyfriend. She said he had the same brown eyes and scruffy black hair, but much nicer manners apparently."

Caroline sighed. She had a feeling she knew exactly what was coming next. Her instincts proved correct when Charlie fixed his bright blue eyes on her and wheedled, "Can we give Freddie a home, Mum? You did promise we could have a dog when we moved to Riverdale because we were leaving all our friends behind. And it would stop me looking for the big cat."

"Charlie and I will look after him and take him for walks," said Poppy, giving her stepmother an imploring look. “You needn’t do a thing. Imagine how awful it would be if no-one else gave him a home? He’d have to spend the rest of his life in a cage.”

Caroline opened her mouth to speak but the vet joined the offensive before she could utter a word. “I know he does look a bit of a state but other than that broken leg there’s nothing wrong with him. And I think he’s probably only about eighteen months old, so he would give you years of pleasure. I’d take him in myself if I didn’t already have four at home.”

“Do we really need another waif and stray? What will your dad say? What will Magpie say?” asked Caroline. But she had to admit the dog really did have the softest brown eyes. Almost as if he could sense her wavering, Cloud gave her a nudge and she turned to the children and laughed.

“OK, OK. I know when I’m beaten. But I’ll hold you to your promise. He can be your responsibility. And you two can break the news to your dad.”

Charlie flung his arms around his mum and Poppy gave her a quick kiss on the cheek. She still felt a little shy around her stepmother but things were so much better between them now. Caroline enveloped her in a hug, ruffled Charlie’s blond hair and gave the vet an ironic smile. “Come on you lot. We’d better say goodbye to Freddie for now and get this X-ray done, before we end up offering a home to any more lame ducks.”

CHAPTER 3

Half an hour later Cloud and Chester were back in the trailer and Poppy and Caroline had joined the vet in one of the consulting rooms. She used a pencil to point at an X-ray, which glowed a ghostly white against the dark background.

"This is his pedal bone. And this is what I was worried about. Can you see the hairline crack? I'm afraid he has fractured the bone." Poppy nodded mutely. A natural pessimist, she had spent the last week fearing the worst, but she took no pleasure in being proved right. Caroline squeezed her hand.

"But it could be a lot worse. There's no wound, which means there should be no danger of infection, and the fracture hasn't reached the coffin joint. That's the joint between Cloud's pedal bone and his short pastern."

"So what happens now?" Caroline asked.

"Box rest is the most important part of the treatment for a fractured pedal bone, and you're already doing that. He'll need two to three months of total box rest. We need to completely immobilise that foot to give the bone the greatest chance of healing. He needs to be fitted with a bar shoe, and if that doesn't work we'll look at applying a cast to his hoof and pastern. With the right treatment the prognosis for a full recovery is very good."

"Is there anything else I can do for him?" Poppy asked.

"No, you carry on exactly as you are. He's already looking so much better than when I saw him on Monday. We'll repeat the X-ray in four weeks' time to see if the bone is beginning to heal and go from there."

When Caroline and Poppy stepped back out into the yard Charlie was leaning against Freddie's cage, stroking the dog's nose through the wire.

"The vet wants Freddie to stay here for a week so she can keep an eye on him. She said we could pick him up on Friday," Caroline told him. "That gives you precisely six days to win your father around."

On Sunday morning Poppy was woken by a bleep on her mobile phone. It was a text from Scarlett.

Hi Poppy, fancy a ride? Thought we could go and say hello to the new people. Be here for ten. C U later, Scar xx.

Poppy yawned and stretched. Magpie, the McKeevers' overweight black and white cat, was curled up in a ball on the end of her bed. He eyed her briefly before tucking his head under one paw and going back to sleep. Poppy jumped out of bed, opened the curtains and was greeted by a crisp autumn morning, the sun low in a bleached blue sky. She gazed down at the stables. Cloud's grey head looked out over the stable door, his warm breath like curls of smoke in the cold air. Poppy opened her window and called softly to him. He saw her and whickered. She calculated that she still had time to spend a couple of hours with him before meeting Scarlett. She threw on some clothes, ran down the stairs and grabbed a plate of toast from Caroline in the kitchen, grinning her thanks as she headed for the back door.

Chester had shouldered Cloud out of the way and it was the donkey she could see over the stable door as she pulled on her wellies. Cloud was at the back of the stable resting his bad leg. Poppy ran her hand over his neck and leant on his withers. His mane tickled her cheek and she sighed with contentment.

She let Chester out into the yard and Cloud watched her muck out the stable, change the water and re-fill the hayrack. "I'm going to give you a groom and then you are going to test me on my German homework. I've got to learn the numbers from twenty to forty by tomorrow otherwise Miss Maher will have my guts for garters," she told him as he started tugging wisps of hay from the rack.

Poppy lost track of time and had to run most of

the way to Ashworthy, where she and Scarlett spent half an hour brushing the worst of the mud from Scarlett's two Dartmoor ponies, Flynn and Blaze. Scarlett had talked her mum into having Blaze clipped but Flynn's winter coat was growing thicker by the day and his mane was bushier than ever. When Poppy bent down to pick out his feet he seized the chance to nibble her pockets. "Do you ever think about anything other than your stomach?" she asked him, rubbing his ear with affection.

Scarlett grimaced as she hauled a rucksack over her shoulder. "Mum's insisted on giving me some chocolate brownies to give to the new people as a moving in present. I told her they'd be broken into a million pieces by the time we get there but she still made me bring them." Scarlett eyed Flynn's round belly, then looked down at her own sturdy legs and sighed. "She thinks feeding people is the answer to everything."

The two girls swung into their saddles and clip-clopped down the farm track to the lane. They turned left, passing the Riverdale drive and heading towards the Blackstone farm at the other side of the valley. The two semi-detached farm cottages were on the Waterby side of the ramshackle farm. Poppy had ridden past them a dozen times without paying much attention. The two white rendered houses, built in the 1950s, were at first glance mirror images of each other. But as they approached she realised the difference was enormous. The cottage on the left sat behind an immaculately manicured front garden whose symmetrical flowerbeds, filled with cyclamens and winter pansies, reminded her of a municipal park. A concrete Greek goddess gazed benignly at them from her plinth in the centre of this kaleidoscope of colour. The windows of the cottage gleamed and a row of white shirts danced in the breeze at the side of the house. Poppy could just make out the navy brass name plate by the front door. Rose Cottage.

The house to the right was more like something out of a Brothers Grimm fairy-tale than a Greek myth. A wooden gate, hanging precariously from rusty hinges, led to a concrete path that was breaking up in places. Brambles and nettles had long taken over the lawn and were now waist high. The wooden window frames were rotten and the windows themselves were opaque with years of grime. A wheelie bin to the side of the front door was painted with the words Flint Cottage. Poppy and Scarlett looked at each other dubiously.

"I'll go. You stay here and hold the ponies," Scarlett offered, much to Poppy's relief. Scarlett was as outgoing as Poppy was shy and although Poppy knew she shouldn't depend on her friend to take charge it was sometimes easier to.

Scarlett edged her way past the nettles and brambles to the front door and pressed a doorbell at the side of the tarnished letterbox. The resulting chime was unexpectedly loud, making her jump. For a while nothing happened and Scarlett was about to press the buzzer a second time when the front door opened an inch.

"Hello?" Scarlett said. "Is there anybody there?"

The safety chain was on and the door opened no further. Scarlett glanced uncertainly at Poppy. She turned back to the house and froze as she saw thin fingers curl around the door jamb. The hairs on the back of her neck stood to attention as a voice whispered, "Who are you?"

CHAPTER 4

Poppy, from her vantage point in the lane, only heard Scarlett's reply.

"My name's Scarlett and my best friend Poppy is just over there. We live next door to each other on the other side of the valley. We heard new people had moved in and wanted to say hello. Oh, and my mum made some brownies for you, though they look more like the broken bits of cake that go at the bottom of trifles now. I knew we shouldn't have had that canter. I tell you what, I'll leave them on the doorstep. We need to get going anyway. You can keep the box they're in – it's only an old biscuit tin. Well, welcome to Waterby. It was nice meeting you, er –"

Poppy caught a murmured answer. The fingers uncurled from the door and it closed with a creak inches from Scarlett's freckled nose. Poppy watched her friend place the tin of brownies on the doorstep and re-trace her steps down the concrete path. When she glanced up at the house again, curious to see what was behind the filthy windows, the face of the girl suddenly appeared. Her huge eyes stared at Poppy for a couple of seconds before she turned and vanished from view.

"Well, that was seriously creepy," said Scarlett, taking Blaze's reins from Poppy. They mounted and turned the ponies for home. Scarlett filled her friend in on the short-lived conversation she'd had with the mysterious girl. "She's called Hope. She said she couldn't let me in because her mum wasn't there. And did you see what a state the house was in? Trust George Blackstone to rent out such a dump. I wouldn't let my worst enemy stay there. But Mum always says he's as tight as they come. I doubt he's spent a penny doing it up for the new family."

Poppy nodded. Blackstone was public enemy number one as far as she was concerned. Five years ago the belligerent farmer had bought Cloud, thinking he was going to make a packet selling the pony on, but when Cloud escaped onto the moor, the farmer had nursed a grudge against him. After the annual drift, the Connemara had been sent back to the Blackstone farm, albeit briefly. Poppy shivered as she pictured the dried blood caked to Cloud's flanks when he'd finally returned to Riverdale. She felt sorry for the newcomers.

As they trotted down the lane Poppy was haunted by the face at the window. The girl had stared at her with such intensity that she felt uncomfortable. Something else wasn't right, she was sure of it. But she had no idea what it was.

"Did you see the girl's face?" she asked Scarlett.

"No, just her arm. She had long, skinny fingers and a red mark on the inside of her wrist. Oh, and she bites her nails. I suppose she'd been told by her mum not to open the door to strangers. Though I hardly look like the Child Catcher from Chitty Chitty Bang Bang. My nose isn't half as long as his for a start…"

The two Dartmoor ponies walked towards home with an easy stride. Poppy let Scarlett chatter on as she mulled over the visit. Every now and then Flynn, sensing that Poppy's mind was elsewhere, seized the opportunity to snatch a mouthful from the hedge. His bay ears were pricked and she felt his pace quicken as they turned into the rutted farm track that led to Ashworthy.

"You're quiet," Scarlett remarked.

"That's because you do enough talking for two, Scar. Only kidding. It's because I'm thinking. There's something about that house – about that girl – that's bothering me. But I can't think what it is."

They untacked the ponies, gave them a brush down, put on their rugs and turned them out in their paddock. Then the realisation hit Poppy like a sledgehammer. She felt prickles of disquiet on the back of her neck. She put her hand on Scarlett's arm and said, "I know what it is about that girl at the Blackstone cottage."

"What?"

Poppy paused. Was it any of her business anyway? But she saw the curiosity on her friend's face and carried on regardless.

"She had no hair."

CHAPTER 5

Charlie spent the week preparing the house for Freddie's arrival. He held impromptu counselling sessions for Magpie, showing him pictures he'd sketched of black and tan dogs and holding the protesting cat up to the television every time a dog appeared on the screen. They went to Baxters' Animal Feeds on the Tavistock road and bought a navy blue dog bed, a collar, lead and water and food bowls. With Poppy's help Charlie cleared the alcove under the stairs of its usual jumble of shoes, bags and coats.

"We can put his bed here. He'll be like Harry Potter at the Dursleys' – sleeping under the stairs. Though he won't be locked in like Harry was. I wonder what happened when Harry needed the loo in the middle of the night?" Charlie pondered.

Their dad watched the preparations with mild amusement. Charlie had been right about him – he loved dogs and was looking forward to Freddie's arrival as much as Poppy and Charlie. He also thought that having a dog in the house would offer extra security for Caroline and the children during his long work trips abroad.

"I don't think Freddie's necessarily guard dog material," Caroline pointed out, remembering the dog's liquid brown eyes and his attempt to shake hands. "He's a big softie."

"Not once I've started his special forces training. I'm going to teach him to kill on command," declared Charlie.

"Don't let Magpie hear you," warned their dad. "You've been telling him all week that dogs are really big friendly cats in disguise."

Charlie grinned unashamedly and held his finger to his lips. "Our little secret, Dad. I won't tell Magpie if you don't." He paused. "Poppy, do you think Freddie and Cloud have already met? They seemed to recognise each other at the vet's."

Poppy thought back. Charlie was right. If Cloud hadn't whinnied she'd have walked straight past Freddie's kennel, assuming it was empty. "I suppose they could have come across each other on the moor. I wonder how long ago Freddie was dumped."

"Long enough for him to need some serious fattening up," said Caroline. "Which reminds me, we need to pop into Waterby after school tomorrow to get some dog food. It's the only chance we'll get before we pick Freddie up on Friday."

Waterby Post Office and Stores was the nerve centre not only of the village but also of the wider rural community. The nearest supermarket was almost ten miles away and the shop was a lifeline for many. It was owned and run by Barney Broomfield, who the McKeevers had nicknamed Father Christmas because of his white beard, twinkly blue eyes, rounded paunch and penchant for red sweaters. They felt it was no coincidence that the only day of the year the shop closed was Christmas Day.

Barney took an eccentric and eclectic approach to ordering stock.

"Oh look, some Big Ben money boxes. Cool!" said Charlie, who was wandering up and down the three aisles while Poppy and Caroline scrutinised the labels on different brands of dog food.

"They're for the grockles, lad," boomed Barney's deep voice from the other side of the shop. "Classy, aren't they? I've some T-shirts with the Queen's corgis printed on the front arriving next week."

"Grockles?" whispered Poppy, looking at Caroline in bemusement.

"It's what people in the West Country call tourists," Caroline whispered back. "Though I'm not sure grockles visiting Dartmoor are going to want corgi T-shirts and Big Ben money boxes." Poppy stifled a giggle.

Then from an aisle behind them she heard a girl's voice.

"But I don't want to do it any more, Mum. You promised me I wouldn't have to when we moved here." The voice was quiet, breathy. Poppy wondered if it was the girl from Flint Cottage.

"Yeah well, things change, don't they babe? Get over it." There was an edge to the woman's voice that made Poppy uneasy. Caroline was busy scooping tins of dog food into the shopping basket one-handed and clearly wasn't listening.

Poppy picked up the basket and followed her stepmother towards the till where Barney stood waiting for them, his hands resting on his vast stomach.

As Caroline paid a woman with blonde highlighted hair scraped back in a ponytail stepped out from the furthest aisle, a small, thin girl scurrying in her wake. They queued behind Caroline. Poppy eyed them from under her long fringe. The woman was wearing leggings, satin ballet pumps and a denim jacket. Her daughter was clad in raspberry pink jeans, a navy parka coat and a dark grey knitted beanie hat that was pulled down low over her forehead. Most of Barney Broomfield's customers wore Barbours and wellies. The two looked out of place.

Caroline noticed the mother and daughter standing behind her and smiled. The woman stared back, her heavily kohled eyes looking Caroline up and down. Then she rearranged her features into a half-smile and gripped her daughter's hand. When she spoke it was with a nasal twang.

"Alright?"

"Have you met Shelley and Hope Taylor? They've moved into George Blackstone's farm cottage," said Barney, as he scanned the tins of dog food. So this was the mysterious Hope, Poppy thought. She looked different wearing a hat.

"How are you settling in?" Caroline asked. "We only moved down from London in the summer but we absolutely love it here, don't we, Poppy?"

Caroline turned to the girl, whose face was solemn as she watched the exchange. "Have you started school here yet, Hope? Poppy goes to the high school in Tavistock and her brother Charlie, who's around here somewhere, goes to Waterby Primary."

Shelley cut across her daughter before she had a chance to reply. "Hope is home-schooled, aren't you, babe?" Hope bobbed her head obediently.

"She has a school at your home? Is it for everyone?" piped up Charlie, who had appeared beside them with a plastic chicken dog toy and a beseeching look in his eye. "It squeaks when you squeeze it," he said. "It'll help with Freddie's special forces training."

Caroline sighed. "Alright then. Give the chicken to Barney. Home-schooled means your mum or dad teaches you at home," she added, smiling at Shelley and Hope. "Why don't you come over for coffee on Saturday?"

Poppy groaned inwardly. She had Cloud and Chester at home and Scarlett next door. She didn't need any more friends. Hope looked about as enthusiastic as Poppy felt. Shelley looked at her daughter's morose face and then at Poppy. "OK, why not? We'll be there about eleven."

On Friday morning Poppy sat with her form in the school hall for the annual harvest festival assembly. Four trestle tables had been placed centre stage behind the deputy head, who was rambling on about the season of mist and mellow fruitfulness while torrential rain hammered an angry beat against the floor to ceiling windows that looked out over the school playing fields. The legs of the tables were splayed under the weight of hundreds of tins of baked beans and packets of rice and pasta, all destined for local pensioners - whether they wanted them or not. Poppy kept looking at her watch but it wasn't making the time go any quicker. As the whole school shuffled to their feet to sing We Plough the Fields and Scatter, Scarlett nudged her. "What time are you picking him up?" she whispered.

"Straight after school. I've got to walk to the vet's and Caroline and Charlie are meeting me there at four. Want to come? We can give you a lift home."

"You bet! I'll text Mum at break and let her know I won't be on the bus."

The rest of the day trickled by as slowly as treacle. When the last bell sounded Poppy and Scarlett couldn't get out of the school gates fast enough. As they walked into the surgery car park Caroline and

Charlie appeared from reception, followed by the vet.

"How's that pony of yours doing? Are you fattening him up nicely?"

Poppy nodded. "He's definitely put on a bit of weight and he's had his shoe fitted. I just hope his foot is getting better."

"Give him time. When we X-ray him again we should get an idea whether it's healing or not. It's a waiting game, I'm afraid."

They heard a woof. "It's Freddie," cried Charlie. "He knows we're here." He ran across the yard to Freddie's cage and poked his fingers through the wire. The dog gave him a friendly lick.

"We'll X-ray Freddie's foot when you bring Cloud over. With any luck they'll both get the all clear. In the meantime Freddie also needs lots of rest. No walks until we know his fracture has healed and you'll need to keep him on the lead when he goes outside to do his business."

"Oh, it's OK," said Charlie, his blue eyes earnest. "We're going to pay for all his food and stuff. He won't need to go out to work."

The vet looked nonplussed. Caroline laughed. "She means when he goes to the toilet, Charlie. Right, shall we let him out?"

Freddie stood as the vet opened his cage. He tottered out on three legs, his feathery black tail swooping back and forth like a windscreen wiper on full speed.

"You were right, Poppy. He's lovely," said Scarlett, giving the dog a pat. "What breed do you think he is?"

"Oh, mainly German Shepherd with a smidgen of border collie, I should think," said the vet.

"So he's a police dog and a sheep dog rolled into one. How cool is that, Charlie?" said Poppy.

"A police dog and a sheep dog. That's epic! He'll be able to track down and round up. We could go out onto the moor and…"

"Charlie! Don't even think about it," warned Caroline. "I'm not having you going after that wretched panther again, with or without Freddie," she added, remembering the danger Poppy and Charlie had faced when Charlie decided to go hunting for big cats while she was in hospital with a broken wrist. Poppy had gone looking for him and the two children had become lost on the moor, sparking a massive rescue operation. "I need to know that you're not going to be pulling any more stunts like that, Charlie."

"It's OK, Mum. I promise I won't."

Caroline produced Freddie's new collar and lead from her handbag. "Here you are, Poppy. You do the honours."

Poppy stroked Freddie's silky ears, eased the collar over his head and clicked on the lead, which she handed straight to Charlie. He whipped a dog treat out of his pocket. Freddie sniffed the treat and took it daintily from Charlie's flat palm, his tail thumping.

The vet watched with satisfaction. "I think you're

all going to get along just fine. I love it when a plan comes together."

Saturday morning found Poppy sitting cross-legged in the corner of Cloud's stable, her history homework on her lap. The pony listened intently as she read extracts from a school textbook on the Roman Empire.

"Did you know that Hadrian's Wall took at least five years to build? And that when Mount Vesuvius erupted the lava flew twenty kilometres into the air? A flock of six hundred sheep was swallowed into a huge crack in the ground. Imagine that! But I've got to write about the Roman army, so I suppose I'd better get on with it. What *is* the difference between a legion and a century?"

Poppy flicked open the textbook to the page on Roman soldiers. She was chewing the end of her fountain pen and contemplating how to begin the essay when a scrabble outside made her jump. She looked up in time to see Magpie heaving his swinging stomach over the stable door. He landed with a heavy thud, picked his way fussily over the straw to Poppy and curled up beside her. She stroked him absentmindedly and was about to begin writing when she was interrupted again, this time by her brother.

"Poppy, they're here!" Charlie announced. "Mum says to come and say hello."

"OK. I won't be a minute." Poppy sighed, gave Magpie's chin a tickle and kissed Cloud goodbye. She followed the brick path around the side of the house and, as she reached the front garden, saw Caroline talking to Shelley while Charlie and Freddie waited by the front door. Hope was standing awkwardly to one side, chewing a nail. She was wearing the same green coat and beanie hat that she'd had on in the village shop. She was so slight she could have blown away in the wind. Poppy's natural shyness anchored her to the spot until Freddie noticed her loitering and woofed a greeting.

"Poppy, there you are! Come and say hello. Why don't you take Hope to see Cloud and Chester while I put the kettle on?" Caroline suggested, leading Shelley indoors.

"Who are Cloud and Chester?" asked Hope.

"Chester's a donkey. He belonged to the lady who used to own Riverdale, but she moved to a flat in Tavistock and couldn't take him with her. We kind of inherited him when we moved here. And Cloud's my pony." Saying the words out loud still gave Poppy a thrill.

Hope's features lit up like a beacon. "You have your own pony? No way! You're so lucky!"

"I still can't quite believe it myself," Poppy admitted with a grin. "Follow me, it's this way."

As they walked around the house to the stables Poppy described how she'd found Cloud running wild on the moor and her desperate attempts to rescue him from the drift. "To cut a very long story short, he ended up at the pony sales where my dad bought him."

Cloud was standing at the back of his stable. "He's nervous around people he doesn't know so don't be offended if he doesn't come and say hello," she told Hope, who hesitated by the stable door.

"I don't think I've ever been this close to a real horse before. There aren't many in Croydon. Big, aren't they?"

Poppy slipped through the stable door and scratched Cloud's forehead fondly. "He's broken a bone in his foot and needs to have complete box rest. That means he's not allowed out of his stable until it heals. He's due to have another X-ray in a fortnight," she explained.

"I would love to learn to ride," said Hope, watching Cloud nuzzle Poppy's pockets.

"I'm afraid no-one can ride Cloud until his foot heals and Chester's too old for riding, so I can't help you there. But I could have a word with Scarlett if you like. She might let you have a go on Flynn. He's a Dartmoor pony. She taught me to ride on him this summer."

"Would you?" said Hope, her pale blue eyes shining. Then her face fell. "I don't suppose my mum'll let me. She'll say it's too risky or something."

"You don't know until you try. Let me speak to Scarlett first."

"Thanks Poppy, you're really kind. But you don't understand what she's like."

CHAPTER 6

The fire in the lounge was crackling, sending sparks shooting up the chimney. Caroline and Shelley were perched either end of the sofa, sipping mugs of coffee. Charlie and Freddie sat on the rug in front of the fire, Freddie's bandaged paw in Charlie's lap. Magpie had retreated to the window ledge, where he eyed the dog with loathing. It was no surprise that Charlie's counselling sessions had not had the desired effect and Freddie's appearance had put Magpie's whiskered nose severely out of joint.

"I've lived in Croydon for most of my life," Shelley was saying. She noticed the girls' arrival and patted the sofa beside her firmly, inviting her daughter to sit next to her. Hope, who had discarded her coat but was still wearing the dark grey beanie hat, sat down, leaving a noticeable gap between them.

"What brought you to Waterby? Caroline asked.

"It's just the two of us these days, isn't it, babe?" said Shelley. "The last year hasn't been great and I thought we could both do with a change of scene."

"Why? What happened?" asked Charlie, his curiosity piqued. Caroline shot him a look but Shelley shrugged her shoulders.

"It's OK, we don't mind people knowing, do we Hope? Last November Hope was diagnosed with leukaemia, weren't you, babe?" Hope nodded mutely. Poppy felt a swooping sensation in her stomach. Caroline looked shocked.

"What's luke…lukema?" Charlie asked.

"It's cancer of the blood. She'd been losing weight and had no energy. We found out after our doctor sent her for tests."

"That's awful," said Caroline.

"Tell me about it. She's spent the last ten months having chemotherapy. That's why she lost her hair." Shelley reached over and pulled off Hope's hat. The way she did it, almost with a flourish, reminded Poppy of a waiter lifting the silver platter from a dish of food. A single tear trickled down the side of Hope's nose.

Her head was completely bald, her pink skin as soft and vulnerable as the snout of a mole. Hope gave her mother a dark look, snatched her hat back and tugged it down over her forehead.

"Alright Hope, don't get narky. I was just showing Caroline and Poppy your hair. Or should I say lack of it. I'm joking! Honestly, where's your sense of humour?"

"How is Hope now?" Caroline asked tentatively.

"Not so good. That's why she's not at school. Her immune system is so weak after all the chemo that she'd catch every infection going if she went to Waterby Primary. The oncologist has told us there's nothing more he can do. But there's a new treatment in America that's having amazing results with Hope's type of leukaemia. I just need to find a way of sending her there and paying for her treatment."

"Crikey, I don't suppose that's going to be cheap," Caroline said.

"I reckon it'll cost about ten grand, what with our flights to San Francisco, accommodation and the treatment itself. There's no way I can afford that. Actually I'm thinking about setting up a fund to raise the money. I might call it Hope for Hope, or something like that."

"What a fantastic idea. We'd help, wouldn't we kids?"

Poppy was still reeling from the news of Hope's illness. She nodded vigorously. "Yes, of course. Scarlett and I could hold a cake sale at school."

"No offence babe, but it'll need more than a cake sale. I could do with a story in the local rag. That's what other families do and it always seems to do the trick."

"What about Sniffer? He'd help," said Charlie.

"He's a reporter on the Tavistock Herald. His real name's Stanley Smith but everyone calls him Sniffer," explained Caroline. "He did a story on Poppy and Charlie when they saw the Beast of Dartmoor a while back. I'm sure he would be interested. I probably have his number here somewhere."

Shelley clapped her hands. Poppy noticed she had a butterfly tattoo on the inside of her right wrist. "I'll give him a call this afternoon. We might be able to go America after all, Hope. Wouldn't that be wicked?"

Hope looked as though it would be anything but. She looked…weary. There was no other word to describe it.

The village of Waterby was still slumbering on Friday morning when a white transit van pulled up outside the Post Office and Stores. Only Barney Broomfield was up, the lights in his shop cheerily bright in the murky half-light. The driver hopped out of the van and hauled out several bundles of newspapers, which he stacked in an untidy heap at Barney's feet. Barney hefted them one by one into the shop, sorting the national newspapers into one pile and the Tavistock Heralds into another, ready for his small band of paperboys and girls. It was a ritual he'd carried out at five o'clock every morning since he took over the shop over twenty years ago. The only lie-in he allowed himself was on Christmas Day.

After all the papers were sorted he made himself a cup of tea and picked up a copy of the Herald. He raised his eyebrows when he read the headline and saw the two faces staring solemnly back at him from the front page. "She's a fast worker, that one," he said to himself, as he took a slurp of tea and settled down to read.

Poppy didn't see the paper until that evening. She let herself in the back door after school and ran upstairs to change out of her uniform. Her dad peered around her bedroom door.

"Hi Poppy, how was school?"

"Fine," she replied.

He came in and sat down on the wicker chair by the window. "Anything exciting happen?"

"Nope."

"Are you settling in OK?"

"Yep."

"Charlie is having tea at Ed's and Caroline has popped over to the farm to pick up some eggs. I'm in charge of dinner."

"Oh, right," said Poppy, impatient to see Cloud after a day apart. She pulled on a fleece top and eyed the door. Her dad sighed and stood up. He had been looking forward to a chat with Poppy. She had virtually moved into Cloud's stable and he couldn't remember the last time they had talked properly.

He tried again. "How's Cloud doing?"

"Good, Dad. He's doing really well," Poppy finally turned her attention to her father. He could feel the happiness radiating from her. He'd taken some convincing to buy the emaciated grey pony at the Tavistock Horse Sales but it had been the right thing to do, there was no doubt. The girl and pony belonged to each other.

"I'm glad. I've got to go to London for a couple of days tomorrow. The car's coming to pick me up at eight. We can drop you off at school on the way through if you like?"

"And Scarlett?"

"Yes, of course." He smiled. "Right, you'd better go and see that pony of yours. We can have a chat in the morning."

"Thanks, Dad," grinned Poppy. She kissed him briefly on the cheek before flying out of the room, her ponytail swinging. She paused on the landing as he called after her.

"Oh, I almost forgot. Caroline said you should have a look at the Herald. It's on the kitchen table."

She grabbed the paper as she raced through the kitchen and out of the back door. Caroline had already brought Chester in from his paddock and the pony and donkey were both watching over the stable door for her.

"I'm sorry," she said. "I'll be two minutes, no longer. I promise." In the tack room Poppy scooped pony nuts, chaff and soaked sugar beet into two buckets. She swung open the stable door, tossed the newspaper into the corner and held out the buckets. "Here you go. Dig in."

While they were eating she mucked out the stable. As she bent down to pick up the grooming kit she noticed the photograph on the front page of the

Herald.

"That's Hope and Shelley!" The pair gazed out below an enormous headline, *Hope for Hope.* She picked up the paper and started reading.

A Waterby mum has launched a £10,000 appeal to send her daughter to America for life-saving cancer treatment.

Brave Hope Taylor was diagnosed with a rare and aggressive form of leukaemia almost a year ago and has spent the last 10 months having chemotherapy.

But the 10-year-old, who moved to Waterby with her mum Shelley earlier this month, faces an uncertain future as the chemotherapy was not successful.

"We've been told that there's nothing more doctors in the UK can do for her," said single mum Shelley, 36.

Her only hope for Hope is a radical new treatment, which is being pioneered by a team of cancer specialists in California.

Shelley has launched a fund to raise money to pay for the treatment. She hopes people will throw their weight behind the appeal, which she has called Hope for Hope.

"We need to reach £10,000 and the sooner the better as Hope is getting weaker all the time," she explained.

"I want people to imagine how they would feel if their only child had terminal cancer. I've set up a special Hope for Hope Facebook page where they can find out more about the treatment and how to make donations -"

Poppy stopped reading and studied the photo. Shelley's arm was draped protectively around her daughter's slight shoulders. Poppy could just make out the butterfly tattoo on her wrist. Hope wasn't wearing a hat and her eyes looked huge in her pale face. Poppy decided there and then that she would do whatever she could to help her new friend get the treatment she so badly needed.

CHAPTER 7

When she'd settled Cloud and Chester for the night, Poppy found Caroline laying the kitchen table while her dad stirred a saucepan on the stove. Charlie was lying on his back waving his legs and arms in the air. Freddie was watching him, his head cocked, a bemused expression on his black and tan face.

"What on earth are you doing, Charlie?" asked Poppy, shaking off her boots and dropping the newspaper on the worktop.

"Teaching Freddie some tricks for the Waterby Dog Show. It's on the second Saturday of half term. Ed's mum told me about it," he replied. "If Freddie's foot's better we're going to enter one of the classes, aren't we Fred?" The dog thumped his tail.

"There's probably something about the dog show in the Herald. Did you see the story about Hope and Shelley?" asked Caroline, as she took four pasta bowls out of the cupboard.

Poppy nodded. Her dad started heaping spaghetti into the bowls, followed by spoonfuls of Bolognese sauce. He called it his speciality dish. In fact it was the only dish he knew how to make. Caroline was definitely the cook of the family.

"What are they like then?" he asked, as he grated parmesan cheese over the four steaming bowls.

Poppy gave her hands a cursory wash under the tap and sat down next to Caroline.

"Shelley is quite -" Caroline paused, searching for a word that wouldn't sound too judgemental. "Single-minded, I suppose you could say. She must be, to go through all that and still come out fighting. Hope's very quiet, isn't she, Poppy?"

Poppy remembered the exchange she'd overheard in the village shop. "Mmm," she replied, through a forkful of spaghetti. "She wants to learn to ride. I told her Scarlett might let her have a go on Flynn but she doesn't think her mum would let her. I suppose she thinks it'd be too dangerous, what with the cancer and everything. I also thought that Scarlett and I could have a go at baking some cakes and if they're any good we could ask Barney if we could sell them outside the shop one Saturday morning to make some money for the appeal."

"That's a lovely idea, sweetheart. Shelley's got her work cut out, raising all that money. Perhaps we can make a donation?" Caroline asked her husband.

"Of course we should. It sounds as though Hope

needs all the help she can get. Now I might sit down with the paper if that's OK with you lot? It's going to be the last chance I get to put my feet up for a couple of days."

Poppy helped Caroline clear the table and they chatted about the weekend. Tory Wickens, the former owner of Riverdale, was coming for Sunday lunch. Since the McKeevers had bought the house she'd become a close family friend. Poppy tried to pop in to see the old woman in her sheltered flat in Tavistock every couple of weeks but it would be good to spend the day together and she was looking forward to showing her how well Cloud was looking.

"Blimey! Looks like Charlie's big cat has struck again," said Poppy's dad from the lounge. He walked into the kitchen, the Herald in one hand, his reading glasses in the other. "Listen to this," he said, perching his glasses on the end of his nose.

"A big cat expert has claimed that the Beast of Dartmoor was responsible for the mutilated body of a sheep discovered near Waterby, the Herald can exclusively reveal.

"The ram's half-eaten body was found in a dense area of woodland on the outskirts of the village by two birdwatchers on Sunday morning.

"The twitchers called police and officers took the body to Tavistock Veterinary Surgery where a post mortem was carried out on Monday afternoon.

"Vet Sarah Brown told the Herald: 'The ram's throat had been crushed, which is consistent with an attack by a large dog

like a Rottweiler or German Shepherd.'

"But when pressed by the Herald Mrs Brown said she could not rule out the possibility that an even larger animal – such as a panther – had attacked the sheep."

Mike paused to check he still had everyone's attention. Poppy and Caroline were sitting at the kitchen table, listening avidly. Charlie was gaping at him, open-mouthed.

"Farmers fearing for the safety of their flocks urged dog owners to keep their animals under control and warned that any dog caught chasing sheep would be shot. But big cat enthusiast John Clancy, who has been tracking the fabled Beast of Dartmoor for the last five years, said he was certain that the ram had been killed by the large black cat seen by two local children near the Riverdale tor last month.

"'Although I have yet to see this majestic animal with my own eyes I am so convinced it exists that I and my fellow members of the Big Cat Society are spending every waking hour trying to track the panther down so we have proof that we have been right all along –'"

"Why can't they leave him alone!" howled Charlie, his arm around an anxious-looking Freddie.

"Don't they realise it's a wild animal, not an exhibit in a zoo?" Poppy added with feeling. When she and Charlie had glimpsed the panther on the tor she'd been in awe of its raw, untamed beauty. She hated the thought of big cat fanatics trying to track it down just to prove the cynics wrong.

"You must promise me you won't go looking for it again. Remember what happened last time," said Caroline, concerned by the fervent expressions on the children's faces.

"Why would I? I'd be as bad as all those men chasing after him if I did. I want him to be free on the moor, not caught by the big cat men or shot by a farmer," said Charlie, tears trickling down his cheeks.

"I know, sweetheart. Don't upset yourself. That big cat of yours knows how to stay out of everyone's way. You and Poppy are the only people to have ever seen him, don't forget. Come on, let's see if we can find anything in the paper about that dog show." Caroline patted the chair beside her but Charlie, his thumb in his mouth, shook his head. He clung briefly to Freddie's warm neck before running out of the kitchen and upstairs to his room.

"Nice one, Mike," Caroline said shortly, pushing back her chair and following Charlie out of the room. Poppy shot her dad a withering look.

He shrugged his shoulders. Sometimes he didn't understand his family at all. "What did I say?"

CHAPTER 8

By the time Mike's taxi drew up outside Riverdale the following morning all had been forgiven. After stowing his overnight bag in the boot he jumped in beside the driver and Poppy slid into the back seat. At the bottom of the Ashworthy drive they picked up Scarlett and the three of them chatted about school all the way to Tavistock. Outside the school gates he gave Poppy a hug. "Be good for Caroline and keep Charlie out of trouble. I'll see you in a couple of days."

She and Scarlett stood and waved as the taxi did a three point turn and accelerated off towards Plymouth. Scarlett linked arms with Poppy and they joined the stream of students walking through the school gates.

"Let's try out our baking skills tonight, shall we Poppy? I could come round to yours after tea. What d'you reckon?"

"Good idea. I keep thinking about Hope. What must it be like, having no hair? And imagine being told that all the chemotherapy was for nothing? But I have to warn you, I'm about as good at cooking as I am at algebra, and that's not saying much."

Poppy snorted with laughter when Scarlett arrived at the back door that evening wearing a Superman apron.

"Yes, well, I didn't want to get my new top dirty. My brother bought it for Dad last Christmas, not that I've ever seen him cooking. It was the only one I could find. Anyway, it's not that funny," Scarlett grumbled, as she unpacked eggs from a carrier bag. "Mum sent these over in case we needed them. We've got a glut at the moment."

Caroline poked her head around the door. "Hello Scarlett! I've left the cupcake recipe on the dresser. Give me a shout if you need anything."

Within a few minutes the kitchen looked like the set of MasterChef. Scarlett lined up bags of flour, caster sugar and chocolate chips from the cupboards while Poppy ferreted around in the fridge for the butter.

"I should have got it out earlier. It's as hard as a rock," she said, giving the butter a hopeful squeeze.

"I'm sure it'll be fine," said her friend breezily. Scarlett's mum Pat was renowned across Dartmoor for her baking skills and her creations usually won first prize in the village show. As a result Scarlett considered herself to be something of a cake connoisseur. Unfortunately she hadn't inherited Pat's light touch in the kitchen. She wiped her hands on the Superman apron. "Right, let's get this show on the road."

Fifteen minutes later Scarlett's freckles were covered by a light dusting of flour and Poppy's jumper was smeared with streaks of egg and butter. She tucked her hair behind her ears and looked dubiously at their cake mixture.

"It looks a bit…lumpy," she said, picking out a shard of egg shell.

"Nah, it'll be fine once it's cooked. Let's spoon it into the cases and stick it in the oven. I think it says twenty five minutes, doesn't it?" asked Scarlett.

"Gives us just about enough time to clear up the kitchen a bit before Caroline sees it," giggled Poppy. How they had managed to use quite so many bowls and utensils to make twenty cupcakes was beyond her.

Just as the timer on the oven started beeping Charlie ran into the kitchen, swaddled in his fleece dressing gown and his hair smelling of shampoo. Caroline followed him in.

"They smell lovely! Can I have one, Mum? I'll clean my teeth again," he promised.

"You two can be our guinea pigs, although I'm sure they'll be delicious," said Scarlett.

But when Poppy lifted the tray out of the oven she

and Scarlett gasped.

Charlie was puzzled. "I thought you were making chocolate chip cupcakes?" he said. "Those look more like dog biscuits!"

"They do look slightly well done," Caroline said. "And are you sure you used self-raising flour?" She picked up the packet. There was silence as they all read the label. Plain flour.

"Oops," said Scarlett, grinning. "I was in charge of flour. My mistake. Shall we try again?"

But Poppy had a thought. She turned to Charlie. "What did you say they looked like?" she asked him.

"Dog biscuits. I bet Freddie would love them," he said. Freddie looked up from his basket and woofed softly. "See?" he added.

"I don't think dogs are supposed to have chocolate, I remember reading it somewhere. But we could have a go at making proper dog biscuits. I'm sure we could find a recipe on the internet," Poppy said.

"We could sell them at the Waterby Dog Show!" said Scarlett. "We'd have a captive audience. We'd sell loads!"

"That's an excellent idea, you two. I'll have a look for some recipes later. Come on Charlie, let's get you to bed." Caroline paused at the door. "By the way, I love the apron, Scarlett. But I'm not sure you fully channelled Superman's powers tonight."

CHAPTER 9

As November approached the Riverdale wood had never looked more beautiful. The cold nights had quickened the transformation of the wood's acid green shades to vibrant autumnal hues. The horse chestnuts had been the first to turn gold and amber, closely followed by the ash and sycamore trees. But as the days raced by even the oaks and beech trees caught up, their leaves a stunning array of burnt orange, saffron and cinnamon.

Four enormous pumpkins in Caroline's vegetable garden were growing plumper by the day, as was Freddie, whose once matted black and tan coat now shone with good health. Charlie, who never let a brush near his own hair, was meticulous about grooming the dog every evening after school. Freddie sat patiently in front of the fire while the six-year-old brushed and combed, preened and primped. Charlie was still deciding which class to enter at the Waterby Dog Show. "I don't think we're going to be able to go in for the agility ones this year," he told his family over dinner on Friday night. "Freddie's leg might not be better in time."

Poppy reached for the Tavistock Herald and flicked through until she came to a report on the forthcoming show. "You could try for the dog with the waggiest tail or the most appealing eyes," she suggested. "Or there's a class for the most handsome dog and another for the dog the judge would most like to take home."

"I'm not entering that one - I don't want the judge taking him home!" cried Charlie, horrified.

"I don't think that's what it means, Charlie. But look, here's a perfect one for Freddie – the best rescue dog. He'd have a really good chance of winning that."

The phone rang and Caroline disappeared into the lounge to answer it. She came back and sat down. "That was Shelley. She's invited us over for coffee tomorrow morning."

Charlie pulled a face. "Do we have to? I'd much rather go and see Ed."

"Yes," she replied firmly. "It won't do you any harm to keep poor Hope company for an hour or so."

Privately Poppy agreed with Charlie. She'd much rather spend the morning with Cloud. And she had a ton of homework to do. But she had a fleeting image of Hope standing alone at the window of George Blackstone's ramshackle farm cottage and felt a tug of sympathy for the girl.

"I don't mind," she told Caroline. "We can tell Hope and her mum about the dog biscuits. They might even like to come to the dog show."

"Thank-you, sweetheart," Caroline said, flashing Poppy a grateful smile. It wasn't so long ago that Poppy had felt alienated by her stepmother, despite Caroline's best efforts to connect with her. These days she basked in Caroline's approval. What a lot of time she'd wasted. She smiled back, her heart as light as a feather. "Anytime, Mum."

Flint Cottage looked slightly less dilapidated than when she and Scarlett had last visited. Someone had hacked down the brambles and nettles in the front garden and the grimy windows had been treated to a perfunctory clean. Poppy and Charlie followed Caroline up the uneven path and watched as she rang the bell. This time Shelley flung open the door.

"Alright? Welcome to the madhouse. Hope's in the front room. Why don't you kids go and find her and I'll put the kettle on."

The children slipped off their shoes. Charlie stopped in his tracks when he clocked the massive flat screen television on the wall in the lounge. It was about three times the size of the McKeevers' aging set.

"I wish we had a telly like that!" he said.

Poppy, meanwhile, had noticed the brown-haired girl sitting curled up on a scruffy armchair in the corner of the room. Her shiny conker-brown bob had fallen forward, hiding her face as she read a book. White wires trailed from her ears to an iPod on her lap. Her head was nodding in time to the music.

Was it Hope? But this girl had a glossy head of hair. She seemed oblivious to their presence.

"Hello?" said Poppy tentatively. The girl didn't react so Poppy tried again, louder. The girl still didn't look up.

"HOPE!" Charlie bellowed at the top of his voice, the sound reverberating around the small, square room. "IS THAT YOU?"

The girl gave a start and looked up from her novel, her eyebrows raised in surprise. Underneath the heavy fringe was Hope's pale face. For the briefest second Poppy saw a look of apprehension – or was it fear – sweep across her features. She took her earphones out, wound the lead around her iPod and closed the book. Her actions were slow and deliberate, as if she needed time to compose herself. And when she looked up again the expression on her face was blank.

"Crikey, your hair grew back quickly," remarked Charlie, heading for a closer look at the television.

"Charlie!" Poppy admonished.

"It's a wig," Hope said in her breathy voice. "My mum sent for it the other day and it arrived in the post this morning. It's made with human hair."

Charlie turned from the television and stared at

Hope in fascination. "What, from a real live dead person?"

"Charlie!" cried Poppy again, her face flushing with embarrassment. Sometimes he had the sensitivity of a gnat.

"S'alright," said Hope, with the barest hint of a smile. "Some people donate their hair to charities that make wigs for people like me. It doesn't come from dead people."

"I like it," said Poppy firmly, trying to make amends for her brother's lack of tact. "It suits you."

Charlie opened his mouth to speak, but when he saw the expression on his sister's face he snapped it shut again.

"What was your hair like before?" Poppy asked, sitting down on the edge of the faded brown sofa opposite Hope.

The girl smiled. Her face was transformed. "It was down to my waist and was as yellow as straw. My dad used to call me Rapunzel. This hair feels a bit weird, to be honest. But at least it makes a change from the hat."

"Where is your dad? Is he dead?" asked Charlie, plonking himself on the sofa next to his sister. Poppy winced and elbowed him sharply in the ribs.

"Ow! What did you do that for! I was only asking!"

"No, he isn't dead. He moved out last summer," said Hope, her voice low. "He and Mum are getting a divorce."

"Do you get to see him very often?" Poppy asked.

"I haven't seen him for over a year. He lives in Canada now with Kirstin, his new girlfriend. My mum won't let me -"

"Your mum won't let you *what?*"

Hope almost jumped out of her skin at the sound of Shelley's voice. No-one had noticed the lounge door open. Hope fell silent, leaving the sentence dangling like a spider on a silk thread, and stared at her mum warily.

"You won't let me go to school. Because of all the germs," she finished lamely.

Shelley's face cleared. "That's right, babe. I can teach you everything you need to know right here. Who needs school anyway? It didn't exactly do me any favours. Do you lot want a drink?"

She was back moments later with three glasses of orange squash which she set down on the coffee table. Hope went to stand up but caught her foot on the corner of a rug and lost her balance. As she put out a hand to steady herself she knocked the tray, which wobbled as dangerously as a ship on a stormy sea. Hope paled as the vivid orange liquid sloshed over the tops of the glasses.

Shelley seized Hope's wrist and pulled the girl towards her. "Look what you've done now, you stupid girl!" she spat.

"I'm sorry, Mum. It was an accident. I'll clear it up."

Shelley twisted Hope's wrist and pushed her towards the door. "Too right you will. Go and get a cloth before it leaks onto the carpet," she ordered.

Remembering that Poppy and Charlie were still in the room Shelley turned to them and forced a smile. But her eyes remained narrowed. "I don't know, how clumsy can you get?" she asked. Poppy picked at a broken nail and said nothing. Even Charlie had been left speechless by the venom in Shelley's voice.

"Right. Well, I'll leave you to it." With that Shelley swept out of the room. Poppy noticed Hope standing just outside the door, holding a cloth in one hand and twiddling nervously with a strand of her copper-coloured wig with the other as her mum passed. She slunk into the room and began dabbing ineffectually at the spilt squash.

"Here, let me do it," said Poppy. She eased the cloth from Hope's thin fingers and wiped up the mess. "There you go, all sorted."

Hope murmured her thanks and folded herself into the armchair.

"Hope –" Poppy began. But the girl turned away. The shutters had come down. The atmosphere in the small lounge suddenly felt oppressive and Poppy was relieved for once when Charlie broke the silence.

"Can we turn on the telly?"

"If you like." Hope stood up, crossed the room and switched on the television. She picked up the remote control and pressed a couple of buttons. Nothing happened. She waved the remote in the direction of the set and kept pressing. The screen remained stubbornly blank.

"Sorry, I haven't sussed out how to work it yet," she admitted.

"Let me have a look," offered Charlie. Hope passed him the remote control. "It's the same as Ed's." Charlie fiddled with the remote and the reassuring face of Sir David Attenborough filled the screen. "Oh cool, a wildlife programme. Can we watch this?" he asked.

Poppy and Hope, each deep in their own thoughts, nodded. Neither girl knew quite what to say to the other so they watched TV without speaking until it was time to go home.

CHAPTER 10

Tory Wickens eased the yellowing newspaper cutting into a clear plastic sleeve and placed it in her handbag, careful not to crease it. She had spent the last hour sifting through a box of papers and photos before finding the cutting buried at the bottom. She hadn't touched the box for years. It held too many memories, some of which were still raw. Tory could look at her wedding photographs with equanimity – it was fifteen years since her husband Douglas had died and in that time her grief had softened and blurred. But she could hardly bear to look at the photos of her daughter, Jo, and her granddaughter, Caitlyn. Since Caitlyn's death she and Jo had barely spoken. Tory ran a hand through her white hair and tried to drag her thoughts away from the hunter trial in Widecombe where Caitlyn and her pony had fallen. The chiming clock on the mantelpiece interrupted her thoughts. Ten o'clock. Her nephew was a stickler for punctuality and would be here any moment to drive her to Riverdale. Tory picked up her bag and her two walking sticks and shuffled to the front door to meet him.

Poppy paced up and down the stable, her hands behind her back, with the air of a Brigadier inspecting his troops. She stopped to pick an errant piece of straw out of Chester's woolly forelock before straightening Cloud's rug for the second time.

"I think you pass muster. In fact you both look gorgeous, even though I say so myself," she told them. She looked down at her fleece top and jeans, now covered in the dust and grime that she'd spent the last hour brushing off Chester and Cloud. "Although I can't say the same for me – I'm filthy. I'd better go and change before Tory gets here. Now you two," she added sternly. "Remember to be on your best behaviour, please."

When she heard a car pull up outside the front door, Poppy ran down the stairs, two at a time, and slid to a halt in the hallway, where Charlie was introducing Tory to Freddie. The dog offered his bandaged paw to Tory.

"It's nice to meet you too, Freddie," she told him. "What a handsome chap you are. I hear that you're going to be the star attraction at Waterby Dog Show this year." The dog thumped his tail and Charlie grinned.

"We've been practising, haven't we, Freddie? I've been watching some of the dancing dogs on YouTube. It's given me lots of ideas."

Caroline and Poppy groaned in unison. Caroline took Tory's coat. "Would you like a cup of tea," she asked.

Tory shook her head. "Tea can wait. I'd much rather see Cloud and Chester first. Poppy can take me, can't you, pet?"

Poppy took Tory's arm and they made their way down the hallway, through the kitchen and out of the back door.

"Are they still sharing a stable?" Tory asked.

"I did try them on their own but Cloud made a terrible racket, calling and kicking the door. I was worried he was going to do himself some serious damage. As soon as I put Chester back in the stable he was OK."

"They always did share, you know. Ever since that first day I brought Cloud home from the horse sales. Caitlyn and I didn't like to separate them."

Tory's reminder that Cloud had been Caitlyn's long before he was Poppy's needled. For the last few weeks she hadn't given Caitlyn a second thought. Tory walked slowly over to Cloud, who was standing behind Chester at the back of the stable. Cloud stood motionless, his brown eyes never leaving Tory's lined face as she placed a hand on the Connemara's forehead. It was such a tender, affectionate gesture that Poppy felt as though she was intruding on an intensely private moment. She tried to concentrate on the back of Tory's hand, but the old woman's papery-white skin, dotted with liver spots, swam before her. Suddenly she saw Caitlyn, crouched low over Cloud's neck as he galloped across the moor, his silver mane and tail streaming behind him. She remembered Tory's words the day she'd told Poppy about the accident. How Cloud would do anything for Caitlyn. How they trusted each other completely. How the pony's heart had been broken the day she died. Poppy shook her head and the picture of Caitlyn and Cloud disappeared.

Tory returned to her side. "Cloud is looking so well, Poppy. You really are doing a super job."

"I don't know, Tory. I don't know anything about looking after a pony. Not compared to you. Or Caitlyn."

"Well, it doesn't look like it to me. Chester's never looked better and it's hard to believe that Cloud has spent the last few years running wild on the moor. Don't do yourself down."

Chester chose that moment to walk over and give his former owner a businesslike nudge. Tory laughed and produced a new packet of Polos from her coat pocket. "Alright Chester, is this what you were looking for? You have the memory of an elephant, my old friend."

At the kitchen table, in front of mugs of tea, Tory ferreted around in her bag.

"I've brought something to show you, Poppy. It's an old newspaper report of Brambleton Horse Show in 2006. Caitlyn and Cloud came first in the open jumping class. You remember the photo I have of the two of them being presented with a red rosette? That was the day it was taken. I thought you might like to see it."

Poppy scanned the article. Phrases like 'huge potential', 'winning streak' and 'unbeatable team' leapt out at her from the faded type. She felt Tory's eyes on her and forced a smile.

"It's excellent, Tory. You must have been so proud of them both," she said, to the old woman's obvious pleasure.

Caroline, busy peeling potatoes at the sink, was the only one to notice the tiny catch in Poppy's voice, but said nothing.

Over lunch the McKeevers filled Tory in on the Hope for Hope Appeal and Poppy showed her the recipe for dog biscuits Caroline had found.

"That poor girl. Pass me my bag would you, Charlie dear? Please give this to Hope's mum with my best wishes the next time you see her, Caroline." Poppy watched as Tory slid a cheque for five hundred pounds across the table.

"Are you sure, Tory? That's an awful lot of money," said Caroline.

"I was going to treat myself to a new washing machine but it can wait. This is much more important. I'd like to do whatever I can to help," the old woman said firmly.

CHAPTER 11

Scarlett's dad, Bill, had once again offered to take Cloud to Tavistock for his next vet appointment. Poppy and Scarlett rode in the front of the Land Rover while Caroline and Charlie sat in the back with Freddie. Scarlett sang along to songs on the radio, making up the lyrics she didn't know, which gave Charlie the giggles. Poppy watched the moor race past the window, her thoughts, as always, dominated by Cloud.

"Do you remember Caitlyn, Bill?" she said in a gap between songs. He nodded.

"What was she like?"

"She was a lovely girl, always smiling. You remember her, don't you Scarlett? She used to babysit you and your brother occasionally when your mum and I were busy lambing."

Scarlett was silent, trying to remember, then

exclaimed, "Yes, I think I do! Did she have long, blonde hair? Almost down to her waist? I used to love it when she babysat! She let us watch whatever we wanted on the telly."

"That's her. It was such a tragedy when she died. The whole village was in shock. Why do you ask, Poppy?"

"Oh, no reason. I just wondered, that's all." Poppy returned her gaze to the window. As they reached the outskirts of town, she felt a flutter of nerves. What if Cloud's fracture hadn't healed? What if it was worse? Caroline, watching from the back seat, read her mind.

"Don't worry, Poppy. I'm sure it'll be good news."

Caroline was right to be optimistic.

"Let's start with Freddie's X-ray," said the vet, as they joined her in the consulting room an hour later. "See here? His bone has knitted together perfectly, just as I'd hoped. We can take his cast off today. I'm sure he'll be glad to see the back of it."

"What about Cloud's?" asked Poppy, although she'd known as soon as the vet had pinned the X-ray to the light box. She could still see a faint crack running down the length of his hoof.

"I'm afraid he's not got the all clear yet. But look, here's the X-ray we took a month ago. There's definitely an improvement. The bone is healing, Poppy. It's just going to take time."

Poppy gave the vet a wan smile.

"I'll see Cloud again in another month and

hopefully his foot will be as good as new. Right, let's take off Freddie's plaster cast."

Caroline looked at her watch. "I promised Bill we'd be finished by now. I'd better go and tell him we're almost ready. Come and find me when you're done here, you two."

Poppy held Freddie's lead as the vet rooted around in her bag for a pair of surgical scissors. Charlie noticed her silver name badge as she bent down to start snipping away at the grubby cast. "Are you the vet who was in the paper talking about the black panther?" he asked suddenly.

"You've got a good memory. Why do you ask?"

"Do you really think that sheep was killed by a dog?"

The vet busied herself tidying away the pieces of plaster. Eventually she looked up. "Look, the last thing I want to do is scaremonger," she hedged.

"You can tell us. We won't tell anyone, I swear. We just want him to be safe. It was me and Poppy who saw the panther on the moor, you see."

The vet was silent for a moment. She had worked for a spell at London Zoo when she'd first graduated and knew exactly what a carcass looked like when it had been mauled by big cats.

"It's OK," said Poppy. "We really won't tell."

"Alright. But this has to remain between these four walls, otherwise the big cat fanatics will start causing mayhem. Yes, I am one hundred per cent certain that the ram was killed by a big cat. It probably was a panther, judging by the size of the teeth marks."

"I knew it!" breathed Charlie. "But why has no-one ever seen him apart from us?"

"I've been wondering about that," admitted the vet. "He might be old, he might be ill. Dartmoor is so vast only a desperate animal would come so close to Waterby to hunt."

Poppy could see her brother was looking tearful and she squeezed his hand. "He looked pretty healthy when we saw him. He'll be OK. Come on, Charlie. We'd better go and find Caroline."

Poppy couldn't get the image of Cloud and Caitlyn out of her mind for the next couple of days. Looking after Cloud had been second nature but suddenly she felt clumsy and inept. As if he sensed her crisis of confidence, Cloud withdrew to the back of his stable. The harder she tried to get things right, whether it was tying a quick release knot or picking out his feet, the more ham-fisted she became. She found herself constantly apologising to the pony.

One evening after school Caroline found her in the kitchen, her head in her hands, staring morosely at a pile of schoolbooks that lay untouched in front of her.

"What's wrong, Poppy?"

"Oh, it's nothing. Not really," she answered evasively.

"Is it school?"

"No. School's fine. Too much homework as usual,

but no change there."

"Have you and Scarlett had a falling out?"

Poppy looked at Caroline as though she was mad.

"Have I done something to upset you?"

Poppy shook her head.

"Is it Cloud?"

"Not really. Well, yes. Sort of." Poppy hid behind her fringe so her stepmother couldn't see her face.

"Come on, sweetheart. You can tell me. What's bothering you?" Caroline smoothed her fringe away.

"It's Caitlyn," she finally admitted.

"*Caitlyn?*"

"She was such a good rider. She and Cloud won loads of competitions together. Did you see that newspaper article Tory showed me? They were an 'unbeatable team'." Poppy sketched apostrophe marks in the air. "When – if – Cloud is ever sound again I'll never be as good as her. I know Scarlett's taught me the basics but I don't know how to do a collected canter, let alone a flying change. I'm worried I'll let him down."

"Don't be so hard on yourself, Poppy. We all have to start somewhere. Don't forget you only began riding in the summer. Look how well you've come on since then."

"But Flynn's a schoolmaster. He looks after me, not the other way around. Cloud hasn't been ridden for years. It'll be like backing a youngster and I don't have the experience to do that. I'll be next to useless."

"Leave it with me," Caroline said firmly, as an idea

formed in her mind.

The next morning Poppy's dad came to find her as she swept the yard. He came straight to the point. "Caroline says you're worried that you're not experienced enough to ride Cloud."

Poppy leant the broom against the stable door and nodded mutely.

"I was going to mention this at Christmas, but it seems silly not to tell you now. When your mum died she left you a bit of money. Not much - a couple of thousand pounds. I was thinking, would you like to use some of it to have some proper riding lessons? While Cloud's stuck in his stable?"

"Dad, are you serious?"

"Absolutely."

"I would love to! Not that Scarlett hasn't been a good teacher, she has. But there's so much I don't know."

"I thought you might say yes. I've already rung Bella Thompson and explained the situation."

"Who?"

"Bella's a friend of Tory's and owns Redhall Manor Equestrian Centre on the Okehampton road. She's the lady I met at the pony sales in Tavistock."

Poppy cast her mind back to the day Cloud arrived at Riverdale. Bella had convinced her dad to buy the emaciated pony and for this Poppy would always be grateful.

"She's quite a character," her dad continued, remembering Bella's hearty handshake and her striking resemblance to Chester. "But she certainly knows her stuff. She says she would be delighted to give you some private lessons. I've booked your first one for Thursday at five."

Poppy flung her arms around her dad and he ruffled her hair. "It was Caroline's idea," he said. "And your mum would definitely have approved."

CHAPTER 12

Poppy spent the twenty minute journey to Redhall Manor trying to calm the butterflies in her stomach. She knew any nerves would be transmitted to the pony she would be riding.

"Don't worry, once you get started you'll be absolutely fine," said Caroline, as they pulled into the yard.

As they climbed out of the car a woman's booming voice ricocheted off the walls of the stable blocks, which lined three sides of the yard.

"Sam! Why is Murphy still in his stable? He should have been turned out half an hour ago. And that hay still needs soaking!"

A boy not much older than Poppy appeared from an open door and scuttled across the yard, disappearing into a stable opposite. Hot on his heels strode a woman in jodhpurs and a quilted jacket, her grey hair covered by a headscarf. She stopped when she saw Poppy and Caroline.

"Hello! I'm Bella Thompson. Mike's told me all about you, Poppy, and of course I know Cloud of old," she bellowed, pumping their hands vigorously.

"I wanted to thank you for everything you did at the pony sales. I don't know what would have happened if Dad hadn't met you there," said Poppy.

"A beautiful pony with a long life ahead of him would have ended up as dog food. We were bidding against the knackerman, after all. It doesn't bear thinking about. Anyway, let's not dwell on such gloomy thoughts. Are you all set?"

Poppy nodded.

"You're going to ride Red Rose. Rosie for short. She's tacked up and waiting in her stable. At least I hope she is. Sam!" she yelled. "Have you done Rosie yet?"

The boy poked his head over the stable door. "Yes Gran, she's all ready. I'll bring her out."

"My eldest grandson," Bella explained. "He's a good boy at heart but he's a terrible daydreamer. He's on another planet most of the time."

The boy shot them a rueful look and led a pretty strawberry roan mare out of the stable. "I'll hold her while you get on," he said, pulling down the stirrup leathers.

Poppy grabbed her skull cap, placed her left foot in the stirrup and swung into the saddle. Rosie was at least a hand higher than Flynn and much narrower than the rotund Dartmoor pony. The butterflies re-appeared with a vengeance.

"We're in the indoor school today. This way," said Bella. Rosie followed her owner obediently towards the door of the school before Poppy had a chance to try any of her aids.

"Rosie is a New Forest pony. They make great riding school ponies because they can turn their hand to anything, whether it's polo, gymkhanas, jumping or dressage. I bred Rosie myself. I still have her dam, although she's retired from the school now."

By now they had arrived in the indoor school. The walls of the floodlit steel-framed building were whitewashed and Poppy noticed the dressage markers A, K, E, H, C, M, B and F painted in black at ground level.

"So, how much riding have you done?" Bella asked.

"I only started at the beginning of the summer. I've been riding my friend's Dartmoor pony. She gave me some lessons at the start and we've hacked out a lot but that's about it. I'm sorry, I don't feel that I know very much at all really," Poppy trailed off.

"No, that's good. It's the riders who think they know it all that are the hardest to teach. By the time they come to me they've usually picked up so many bad habits it's almost impossible to re-educate them. Never apologise for wanting to learn, Poppy. Right, I'd like you to walk Rosie around the school on the right rein please."

Poppy gathered up her reins and squeezed her legs

gently. Rosie responded immediately and started walking clockwise around the school. Her stride was much longer than Flynn's and Poppy tried to sit as deeply in the saddle as she could.

"A good rider has a feel for their horse. Good balance is vital," said Bella, watching her appraisingly. "Relax your arms, Poppy. They look like they're glued to your sides. You need to keep the contact with Rosie's mouth but I don't want you looking like a robot."

Poppy tried to relax her arms, her eyes fixed on Rosie's roan ears.

"Look ahead, Poppy, not down at Rosie. That's better. I want you to sit tall in the saddle. Imagine someone's tied a balloon to your head and grow taller from the waist up. Right, change rein diagonally from M to K and at F I'd like you to ask Rosie to trot."

Poppy had just passed H. Used to Flynn's strong mouth and laidback attitude to schooling she started tugging her right rein at M, aiming for the diagonal. Rosie gave a couple of shakes of her head and flicked her tail in displeasure.

"Don't yank at her reins, she has a soft mouth, Poppy. You should use each of your legs and hands when turning. Your inside leg creates impulsion and your outside leg controls the pony's hindquarters. Use your inside hand to ask her to bend and guide her direction and your outside hand to control the amount of bend and impulsion. Does that make sense?"

Poppy nodded.

"Right. Let's try again when you reach F. I want you to change rein from F to H. As you are preparing to turn you should look in the direction you want to go. Put a light pressure on your inside rein. This will warn Rosie that you are about to ask her to turn. Keep your inside leg on the girth and your outside leg just behind the girth and when you're ready ask her to turn with your inside hand and squeeze your legs. You want Rosie to bend with her whole body, not just her neck. That was much better. When you're ready ask her to trot."

Poppy squeezed with her legs and Rosie started to trot.

"Sit for a few strides until you feel her rhythm change then you can start to rise. Keep your hands nice and still and keep a light contact with Rosie's mouth. Very good, Poppy. Slow to a walk at K and I'd like you to change rein on the diagonal again from H to F."

As she walked around the school Bella kept talking. "A transition from trot to walk needs to be ridden just as positively as walk to trot to keep the pony's impulsion. Maintain your contact on the reins and sit for a few strides before you ask her to walk. When you are ready apply pressure to the reins. Make it firm but don't tug. Sit up tall and deep in the saddle and squeeze your legs so her back end doesn't trail and you bring her quarters under. You can give her a slightly longer rein once she's walking but you must maintain contact and impulsion."

For the rest of the hour Poppy practiced her transitions from walk to trot and back again under Bella's eagle eye. Once she started using her aids correctly Rosie proved herself a willing and responsive ride. At the end of the lesson Bella gave the pony a pat and smiled at Poppy.

"Well done. You've a lot to learn but you have a natural balance and, more importantly, you listen. Having the right attitude is what'll help you become an accomplished rider, Poppy. Same time next week?"

Poppy floated back to the car and on the journey home gave Caroline a minute by minute account of the last hour, forgetting that her stepmother had watched the whole lesson.

When she finally stopped talking Caroline said, "I'm glad you enjoyed it so much. Listen, I've had an idea that I wanted to run past you."

Poppy was silent as her stepmother outlined her suggestion. As far as Poppy was concerned it was a no-brainer.

"It's a great idea, Mum. I wish I'd thought of it myself," she said.

The minute the car had crunched up the Riverdale drive she raced around the side of the house to see Cloud.

"I rode a mare called Rosie who's about as big as you. She's lovely, though not as perfect as you, obviously. I'm already learning loads, Cloud. We did transitions from walk to trot today and next week

Bella said we might try a canter. You know all this stuff already, of course." Poppy pictured Caitlyn and Cloud flying over a brightly-painted show jump but she pushed the thought aside. "I'll keep going until I'm as good as Caitlyn," she whispered into his mane.

CHAPTER 13

At the weekend, Caroline insisted on popping into Flint Cottage to see Shelley on their way home from the supermarket.

"I've got a bag of clothes Poppy's grown out of and I wondered if they'd be any good for Hope," said Caroline to Shelley when she answered the door.

"Oh, thanks. Have you got time for a quick cuppa?"

Shelley was wearing her blonde hair loose around her shoulders and she'd swapped her trademark leggings and denim jacket for a pair of skinny jeans that looked brand new, shiny leather boots and a fitted checked jacket. Funny, thought Poppy. It was exactly the kind of outfit Caroline wore.

"You look great. New hairdo?" Caroline asked as she followed Shelley into the kitchen.

"Yeah. Thought I'd treat myself. Hope's moping in her room, Poppy. Honestly, she's as miserable as sin. Perhaps you can cheer her up."

Hope's bedroom was little more than a box room at the back of the house, overlooking the overgrown back garden. The only furniture apart from the bed was a chipped white melamine bedside cabinet and a matching bookcase. The magnolia walls were bare apart from the occasional scuff mark and the faded red curtains clashed with the fuchsia pink duvet cover and the threadbare green carpet. Poppy pictured her own bedroom at Riverdale. Twinkling fairy lights over a wrought iron bedframe, walls covered in her favourite horse posters and a patchwork blanket, knitted by Caroline, on the end of her bed. Hope's room, by comparison, felt unloved. Much like Hope herself, Poppy thought.

"It's not as nice as your room," said Hope, reading her mind.

"Don't be silly, it's a great room," Poppy lied. "And look at the view from your window. You can even see the moor."

Hope sat on the end of her bed while Poppy investigated her collection of pony books. She was impressed. There were dozens of tattered Pullein-Thompson, Ruby Ferguson, Patricia Leitch, Elyne Mitchell and Monica Edwards novels as well as a stack of more modern books.

"Wow, you've got loads more than me."

"My dad used to get them for me. He was always

looking in charity shops and car boot sales and bought anything with a horse or pony on the cover because he knew I'd love it. He always said his best find was this one. It only cost him twenty pence at a boot fair." Hope reached for a hardback book of short stories and gave it to Poppy.

As she flicked through the pages she yelped.

"What's wrong?" asked Hope.

"Nothing, just a paper cut." They both watched as a drop of dark red blood oozed from the pad of Poppy's right index finger. "I don't suppose you have any plasters?"

"Yes, there should be some in the bathroom cabinet. Help yourself."

The bathroom was at the top of the stairs. Poppy could hear Shelley and Caroline chatting in the kitchen below. She wound a piece of toilet roll around her finger, holding it in place with her thumb while she opened the door of the bathroom cabinet. There was the usual jumble of lotions and potions: antiseptic cream, eyewash, indigestion tablets, cotton wool and a couple of packets of painkillers. Poppy found a small box of plasters tucked between a can of shaving foam and a packet of razors. She took one out, threw the now blood-stained piece of toilet roll in the overflowing bin and stuck the plaster on clumsily with her left hand.

At the top of the stairs Poppy paused to listen to Shelley and Caroline.

"I think country life must be agreeing with Hope.

She looks so well," Caroline was saying.

"Whaddya mean?" Shelley answered sharply.

"Oh, only that she has more colour and she's put on a bit of weight. She seems to be thriving."

Shelley made a noise that was somewhere between a harrumph and a tsk. Poppy cocked her head so she could hear the reply. Shelley's tone was reproachful. "The oncologist did say Hope would feel a lot better once the final dose of chemotherapy was out of her system. He told us to make the most of this time because it would be the calm before the storm."

"Of course. How tactless of me. But actually, I wanted to talk to you about that. Poppy's started having riding lessons at Redhall Manor and we were wondering if Hope would like to join her."

"Riding lessons? Why on earth would Hope want riding lessons?" Shelley scoffed. "There's no way I'm forking out for that."

"We thought that after all she's been through it would give her something positive to focus on. And there's no need to worry about the cost. I spoke to the woman who runs the riding school yesterday and explained about Hope. Bella's read all about the appeal in the Herald. She said she would waive the cost of Hope's lessons. In fact she insisted on it. She's brilliant with beginners. Poppy is having lessons every Thursday evening from five until six. I can pick Hope up and drop her off home afterwards. I told Poppy not to mention it to Hope just in case you thought it wasn't such a good idea. Have a think and let me know."

"For free you say?" There was a pause as Shelley considered the offer. Poppy crossed her fingers. "Oh OK, if it's not going to cost me anything, why not? Don't look a riding school gift horse in the mouth, that's what I say."

Poppy could hear Shelley titter at her own joke as she turned and headed for Hope's room.

"All sorted," she announced, holding up her finger to show Hope the plaster. "And I know I should probably wait until your mum tells you but I can't. You know how desperate you are to learn to ride? I've got some news."

CHAPTER 14

The week dragged slowly as Poppy counted the days until her next riding lesson. They picked up Hope on the way. She was quiet on the drive to Redhall Manor, which Poppy put down to nerves. Dressed in Scarlett's hand-me-down jodhpurs and black jodhpur boots and an old quilted anorak of Poppy's, Hope stood awkwardly when they arrived at the riding school.

Sam was nowhere to be seen but Bella was tacking up a chestnut Dartmoor pony slightly smaller than Flynn but no less wide of girth.

"Hello Poppy! And Hope, I presume? I'm Bella. Pleased to meet you, dear. I'm so glad you could come. This is Buster. I thought he'd be perfect for you."

Poppy noticed a dull flush creep up Hope's neck. It must be hard when everyone thought you were a charity case, she thought. But still, no-one in their right mind would turn down free riding lessons with the indomitable Bella Thompson.

"Rosie's in her stable, Poppy. I'd like you to have a go at tacking her up for me while I get Hope started. The tack room's the last door on the left."

Once Bella had found Hope a skull cap that fitted she checked Buster's girth, pulled down his stirrups and showed Hope how to gather her reins in her left hand, place her left foot in the stirrup and swing into the saddle. While she talked Hope through the correct riding position Poppy walked the length of the yard to the tack room. It was a long, narrow room with a small window at the far end. One wall was covered with saddles on red racks. Hanging below each saddle was the corresponding bridle and above was a small wooden plaque showing each horse or pony's name. Poppy breathed in the heady mix of leather and saddle soap.

"Rosie's saddle is the last but one on the end," said a voice, making her jump.

Sam was standing in the doorway, an empty bucket in one hand, a muddy headcollar in the other.

"Sorry, I didn't mean to startle you," he added, dumping the bucket on the ground and lifting the lid off one of the metal feed bins.

"You didn't. I was miles away," she said, watching him deposit a scoop of nuts into the bucket. "Bella's asked me to tack up Rosie. I'm used to tacking up my friend's pony but I'm not sure how to do Rosie's martingale."

Sam pushed his blond fringe out of his eyes and grinned. "She does have high standards, does my gran. I'll show you if you like. You make a start. I won't be a minute."

Poppy found Rosie's saddle and bridle and let herself into her stable. The mare turned to watch her, her pretty roan head still as Poppy undid her headcollar. Poppy, determined to make a good impression, was suddenly all fingers and thumbs. How annoying, she thought crossly. She tried to ease the snaffle bit into Rosie's mouth but the pony, sensing her hesitation, clamped her teeth shut and refused to accept the bit.

"Come on Rosie, there's a good girl," Poppy encouraged, clicking her tongue hopefully. But the pony's mouth remained stubbornly closed.

She became aware of Sam's head over the stable door. She wasn't sure how long he'd been watching her futile attempts.

"Rosie's a great pony but she can be a bit of a moody mare sometimes, especially when she's in season. Would you like me to try?"

"No, I'm alright thanks," Poppy muttered. She took the bridle in her left hand again and held the bit to Rosie's mouth with her right hand. This time, as if sensing her resolve, Rosie opened her mouth obligingly and Poppy brought the headpiece over her ears before she had a chance to change her mind. "There."

Poppy watched as Sam placed the neckstrap of Rosie's running martingale over her head then slipped her girth through the loop on the other end. He unfastened the reins and fed each end through a ring of the martingale before buckling the reins back up. He worked quietly and efficiently and when he finished he gave the mare's forehead an affectionate rub.

"Have you ever heard the saying, 'You can tell a gelding, ask a mare, but you must discuss it with a stallion'? Gran uses it all the time."

Poppy shook her head.

"I prefer working with mares. They are more temperamental for sure, but when you find a mare you click with she'll go to the ends of the earth for you."

"Do you have your own pony or do you just ride the ones in the school?" asked Poppy, suddenly curious.

"Yes, I have a black Connemara mare called Star."

"I have a Connemara, too. He's dappled grey. He's got a fractured pedal bone and is on box rest at the moment. He hasn't been ridden for years. That's why I wanted lessons with your gran. Talking of which, I'd better go. Thanks for the help."

Poppy led Rosie out of the stable, checked her girth, pulled down the stirrups and swung into the saddle. Bella was leading Buster and Hope into the indoor school and she cast her eyes over Rosie's tack as Poppy joined them. "Good job. Now are you both ready?"

Poppy grinned at Hope and they both nodded.

"I'm going to lunge Hope and Buster while you work on your transitions, Poppy. I want you to think about your impulsion and keeping those transitions smooth and balanced."

Poppy was so absorbed in the lesson that the hour flew by. She sat tall in the saddle and tried to give Rosie clear instructions when she wanted to walk or trot.

"Rosie was going well for you today, Poppy. Well done," said Bella. Poppy beamed with delight.

On the way home the girls chatted to Caroline about their lesson.

"I think Sam likes you, Poppy," said Hope out of the blue.

"What?"

"He spent the whole hour watching you. He was standing by the door. Didn't you see him?"

Poppy had been so engrossed in her lesson that she hadn't noticed. She fidgeted uncomfortably in her seat and wound down the window.

"What's wrong, Poppy. Are you feeling car sick? Do you want me to pull over?" asked Caroline, looking at her in the rear view mirror.

"No, it's a bit stuffy in here, that's all. I'm fine." Poppy could see her own reflection in the mirror. Her face was flushed. The car's heating must be on overdrive.

She turned to Hope and replied as nonchalantly as

she could. "Don't be ridiculous, he was watching Rosie, not me."

Hope shrugged. "If you say so."

CHAPTER 15

Poppy and Scarlett met several nights after school the following week to bake batches of dog biscuits for the Hope for Hope Appeal. Caroline had chanced upon a bone-shaped biscuit cutter nestling between a pile of Kendal mint cakes and boxes of fishing tackle in the village shop and the girls used it to cut dozens and dozens of dog-friendly treats. After a couple of burnt batches they had finally – with Caroline's help – got their biscuit-baking down to a fine art. It was torture for Freddie, whose gaze never wavered from the growing piles on the kitchen table.

The day of the dog show was dry and bright, the sun low in a powder blue sky. The show was being held south of the village in a field normally grazed by black-faced sheep. A show ring had been roped off and cars lined the perimeter. As the McKeevers' car bumped through the gate Charlie exclaimed, "I've never seen so many dogs in all my life. They're everywhere!" He was right. Dogs of all sizes, from German Shepherds to miniature dachshunds, strained on leashes or sat patiently while their owners chatted. Poppy watched, fascinated, as an over-excited West Highland terrier raced three times around its middle-aged owner, its lead coiling around the man's tweed-clad legs like a boa constrictor. Blissfully unaware, the man turned to move. He would have fallen flat on his face if it hadn't been for a passing marshal, who shot out a steadying arm just in time.

The McKeevers were directed to their pitch and Caroline parked their estate car next to the dry stone wall that marked the edge of the field.

"Scarlett said she would meet us here. Her dad and Meg are giving a sheepdog demonstration later," said Poppy, as she helped Caroline unload a trestle table and four folding camping chairs from the boot of the car. They had cut long trails of ivy from the hedge at the back of the stables to decorate their sage green table cloth which Poppy arranged with the cellophane bags of dog biscuits as artfully as she could. She had photocopied and laminated the Tavistock Herald's story about Hope's fundraising appeal and was just taping it to the front of the table when Scarlett arrived.

"Hi Poppy! The table looks great. I love the ivy. What a good idea. And the biscuits look delicious. But we still haven't decided how much we are going to charge," she said, without drawing breath.

"Why don't you ask people to make a donation to the appeal in return for a bag of biscuits instead of charging a fixed price? You might find that people will give more," suggested Caroline.

"And we could chop a few biscuits up into little pieces to offer as samples. Just to get them interested," said Poppy.

As a marketing strategy the free samples did the trick and soon a small knot of people, dogs in tow, had gathered around. Scarlett may have been a liability in the kitchen but she was a natural saleswoman.

"I can't think of a better cause. It's so important for Hope to get to America," she told people, watching with satisfaction as they ferreted around in purses and wallets to find five and ten pound notes which they readily exchanged for a bag of home-made dog biscuits.

Poppy was serving a customer when Scarlett nudged her and said, "Look, there's Hope and her mum." She looked up and saw Shelley striding towards their table, Hope a couple of paces behind, her slight frame wrapped in a knee-length padded coat and her head bare.

"How's it going?" Shelley asked, her eyes roving over the table, taking in scattered crumbs and the remaining bags of biscuits. Poppy watched Shelley's eyes linger on the jar of money in front of Scarlett. It was stuffed full of notes. The last time they'd checked they'd counted more than two hundred and fifty pounds. Poppy had been staggered at people's generosity.

"I thought we could sit Hope behind the table to see if she can drum up a bit of extra business," Shelley said.

Caroline looked appalled. "Are you sure she wants to?" she asked faintly. But Shelley appeared not to have heard and prodded her daughter forcibly in the back. "Well, go on then! Go and sit down next to Poppy. I'm going to get a cuppa." With that she turned on her heels and disappeared in the direction of the refreshment tent.

"Why aren't you wearing your new wig, Hope? Your head must be freezing," Charlie said.

"My mum told me not to. She said we'd make more money for our trip to America if people could see my bald head," the girl answered. Poppy felt doubly sorry for her. Imagine having cancer and a mum like Shelley. Life really threw some people a curve ball.

But Shelley was right. People were now happily handing over twenty pound notes for one bag of dog biscuits with their faces full of concern, wishing Hope a speedy recovery. The girl's pale face was flushed with embarrassment as she mumbled her thanks. Poppy knew exactly how she felt – she would have hated the attention, too.

By ten to twelve the girls had completely sold out. A quick count up revealed that they had made just over four hundred pounds in less than three hours. Poppy and Scarlett high-fived each other, whooping with pleasure. Hope sat watching them, an unreadable expression on her face.

Caroline had walked Charlie and Freddie to the show ring as the best rescue dog class was due to start at noon. There was no sign of Shelley.

"Come on, let's go and watch Charlie and Freddie. He'd never forgive us if we missed their big moment. Do you want to come with us, Hope, or stay here and wait for your mum?" said Poppy.

"I'll come if that's OK?" Hope answered diffidently, her thin arms crossed and her shoulders stooped. Her whole demeanour appeared apologetic. Not for the first time Poppy thought how different she was from the brash Shelley.

Hope followed the two friends to where Caroline was watching Charlie and half a dozen other people walking their dogs around the show ring.

Charlie's face was the picture of concentration, his eyes fixed firmly ahead as he followed the elderly woman in front of him, Freddie trotting obediently by his side. After a couple more circuits of the ring the judge motioned everyone to line up with their dogs. He worked his way along the line, chatting to the owners and assessing their pets. Scarlett, who went to the Waterby Dog Show every year, was giving Caroline and Hope a running commentary.

"Look, he's checking that dog's conformation now," she said, as the judge ran a practised hand over a shivering brindle and white whippet, its ears flat and its tail between its legs. Freddie, who was standing two dogs down, looked totally at ease, his pink tongue hanging out and his feathery tail wagging nineteen to the dozen.

Suddenly Poppy spied Shelley standing on the far side of the ring. She was about to tell Hope but something made her pause. Shelley was talking animatedly to a grey-haired man wearing corduroy trousers and a brown hacking jacket that had seen better days. He was in his early sixties, Poppy estimated. He had the sort of puffed out chest and arrogant expression that reminded her of a cockerel. Shelley pointed to the McKeevers' car. The old man looked over and broke into a wheezy laugh that soon turned into an almighty coughing fit that seized his whole body, the convulsions bending him double.

"Who's that man Shelley's talking to?" Poppy whispered to Scarlett.

Poppy watched her friend's face cloud with confusion.

"It's George Blackstone!" Scarlett exclaimed, her voice low. They watched as Shelley patted the spluttering old man gently between the shoulders. But when she saw the two girls watching her Shelley stepped smartly away from Blackstone, pretending to watch the dogs in the ring.

"Are you thinking what I'm thinking?" said Poppy.

"It's a bit strange," admitted her friend. "They look far too cosy for a landlord and his tenant."

Poppy was still puzzling over the possibility that Shelley and George Blackstone knew each other of old when she heard a shriek and a volley of excited barking from the ring. She looked over to see the judge handing Charlie a small silver cup before bending down on one knee to fix a red rosette to Freddie's collar. Caroline, Hope and Scarlett were cheering and Poppy joined in as her brother and Freddie trotted around the ring together, both grinning from ear to ear.

"Did you hear what the judge said?" gabbled Charlie as he re-joined them. "He said Freddie was the bestest rescue dog he'd ever seen and he was the winner by a mile. I can't believe it! We didn't even get a chance to show our latest trick."

They watched as Charlie stood in front of Freddie and commanded, "Roll over!" He smiled with satisfaction as the dog lay down, rolled over and sat up again, his tail wagging.

Poppy hadn't noticed Shelley return. She was talking with Caroline.

"We need to make a move. Things to do. People to see. You know how it is. I'll take the money now then, shall I?" she said.

"Oh, yes, I guess that makes sense, although I've got to go into Tavistock on Monday. I can easily pay it into the Hope for Hope Appeal account at the bank for you," Caroline offered.

"No, you're alright. I'll have it now thanks."

Caroline had locked the money in the car and Poppy watched as her stepmother and Shelley walked over to get it. As if she sensed Poppy's eyes on her retreating back Shelley turned and shot her a look. Her face was hostile and there was an expression in her eyes that Poppy couldn't place. It was only as she lay in bed that night, mulling over the day, that she realised what it was.

Defiance.

CHAPTER 16

Poppy's dad flew out to Syria on the Monday of half-term. During the three week trip he would be responsible for sending daily reports back to London on the crisis in the Middle East. His taxi turned up after breakfast and Poppy, Caroline, Charlie and Freddie lined up outside the front of the house to wave him off. He shook the dog's paw and hugged Poppy and Charlie before wrapping his arms around Caroline, holding her close. Poppy looked down at her feet, not wanting to see Caroline's face. Her stepmother always looked a bit weepy when her dad left for an assignment and Poppy was worried it would set her off. She used to feel utterly desolate when he was away. These days, now she and Caroline were so much closer, she didn't feel as alone as she used to, but she still missed him deeply. It was hard when the only time she saw him was on the six o'clock news.

When the taxi had disappeared down the Riverdale drive Poppy scooted around the side of the house to the stables. Today was an important day. She had decided to try to tack Cloud up for the first time. She'd discovered his old saddle and bridle at the back of the tack room soon after they'd moved to Riverdale, but had assumed it had belonged to Tory's old mare, Hopscotch. Festooned with dusty spiderwebs, the leather was cracked and brittle with age.

"No, that's for Cloud," Tory had said, when Poppy had shown her. "I should have thrown it away. It's Caitlyn's saddle and bridle. We had them specially made for Cloud. I don't like to think of you using them, Poppy. What if they bring bad luck?"

But Poppy, who wasn't afraid to walk under ladders and never worried about spilling salt, dismissed Tory's fears as irrational. Caroline ordered a specialist leather cleaner and conditioner from the internet and Poppy spent hours working on the leather until it felt supple under her fingers.

Cloud was still finishing his breakfast. Poppy mucked out his stable and re-filled his water bucket while he ate. Despite wearing a stable rug his winter coat was thick and she spent the next half an hour giving him a brisk groom, chatting away to him all the while. She felt a flutter of nerves as she wondered how he would react to wearing tack. The last time he'd been ridden was at the hunter trial when Caitlyn was killed. Poppy held his head in her hands and gazed into his brown eyes.

"Do you remember that day, Cloud? The day you fell and Caitlyn died?" she said softly. He turned his head to look out of the stable door at the sound of Caitlyn's name, as if expecting her to stride in, her long, blonde hair swinging, and her skull cap under her arm. Poppy fought the usual feelings of jealousy and inadequacy and wondered if she would ever have enough self-confidence to believe she was equal to Caitlyn.

"I'm here, Cloud," she whispered. "I know you miss Caitlyn but you mean everything to me. You are my world."

He turned and whickered and she felt her heart swell with love.

"Here goes. I promise I'll stop if you don't like it," she said, reaching for the bridle. Cloud had never been head shy with Poppy and as she unfastened his headcollar she ran her hands over his head, giving his poll a scratch and kissing his nose. She held the bridle and eased open Cloud's mouth. Unlike Rosie he accepted the bit straight away and Poppy slid the headpiece over his ears as if she'd been doing it all her life. "You clever, clever boy," she told him.

Poppy lifted the saddle from the stable door. She showed it to Cloud and let him sniff it. She felt his muscles tense as she placed it gently on his back. She watched his face for a reaction. His ears twitched back and forth but he didn't move. She reached for the girth and buckled it up loosely. Cloud remained still. He looked different in his tack. Taller, more imposing somehow. All she wanted to do was jump on his back and gallop across the moor, just the two of them, Poppy and Cloud. Instead she flung her arms around his neck and buried her face deep in his mane. She felt certain that the day would come. She just had to be patient.

"Shelley's asked us to have Hope for the day on Saturday. She's got to go to London to see Hope's oncologist," said Caroline that afternoon.

"On a Saturday?" Poppy was sceptical.

"That's one of his clinic days, apparently. Shelley's going to drop her off early and then drive up to town. She's hoping to be back just after tea."

An orange sun was peeping over the horizon when Shelley's car accelerated up the Riverdale drive, sending gravel flying. Shelley left the engine running as Hope let herself out. Poppy, watching from the lounge window, heard Shelley bark an instruction to her daughter. Hope nodded obediently, her shoulders hunched. Poppy waited until the car had disappeared down the drive before she opened the front door and let Hope in. She had no desire to see Shelley.

The temperature had plummeted overnight and the grass in the paddock was stiff with frost. Hope helped Poppy muck out and feed Cloud and Chester and Poppy showed her how to groom the old donkey before they turned him out.

"Shall we show Hope the Riverdale tor?" asked Charlie, when they finally went inside, their hands red with cold.

"That sounds fun. It's where you saw the big cat, isn't it?" said Hope.

She was wearing her wig and in the warmth of the kitchen her cheeks were rosy. No-one meeting her for the first time would ever have guessed she was in remission from cancer, thought Poppy.

"How's the appeal going, Hope?" asked Caroline. The Herald ran a story every week about the latest fundraising events. It seemed that the people of Waterby had taken the girl's plight to their hearts.

"OK, I think. But Mum deals with all that. I try not to think about it." Hope looked far from pleased at the prospect of a life-saving trip to America. But then who would, thought Poppy. It would be nothing but tests, scans, treatments and more tests. Hardly what you'd call a holiday.

The three children let themselves out of the back gate and began the steep climb to the top of the tor. Conversation petered out as they negotiated rocks and tussocks, Freddie bounding along beside them. Hope was soon breathing heavily. She stopped, wincing as she clutched her side.

"Are you OK?" Poppy asked in alarm.

"It's a stitch. I'm fine. Just unfit I guess," she replied.

Eventually they reached the rock where Poppy and Charlie had seen the panther months before. Charlie went down on hands and knees to show Hope exactly where the big cat had stood. Poppy sat on a wide, flat boulder and looked back at Riverdale. She could just make out Chester grazing in his paddock. From this distance he was the size of the toy donkey in Charlie's farm set. Hope sat down beside her, her knees drawn up under her chin, her wig slightly askew.

"The view from here's amazing. There's Riverdale and Ashworthy, and if you look over there you can just see the roof of the Blackstone farm. And I think that white building to the left of it is your house. Can you see it?"

Hope nodded. They watched Charlie scouting for rocks which he was using to build his own cairn, a scaled down version of the mound of rocks at the top of the Riverdale tor.

"Do you mind if I ask you something, Hope?" Poppy asked. With Shelley safely two hundred and fifty miles away in London it was the first time she'd felt able to tackle the subject. Hope didn't answer so Poppy ploughed on. "The day we first met you and your mum in the village shop, I heard you telling her that you didn't want to do something any more. What was it?"

Hope was silent.

"Is she forcing you to do something?" Poppy faltered. It sounded crazy even thinking it. But she was worried something was wrong. "Is she…hurting you?" she finished lamely.

Hope shook her head vigorously, leaving her wig

even more lopsided.

"No, it's not that," she whispered.

So there was something, Poppy thought. But what?

Hope was quiet for a beat. When she spoke her voice was a monotone. "I don't know what to do. After the last time she promised me it would never happen again. But she was lying."

"Lying about what? I can't help unless you tell me, Hope," said Poppy.

Hugging her knees to her chest Hope turned to face her friend. Tears were streaming down her face and there was a look of such despair in her eyes that Poppy was momentarily lost for words.

"You'll hate me if I tell you, Poppy. You all will."

"Don't be silly, of course we won't. You can trust me. I promise."

Hope took a deep breath, about to speak. But before she had a chance to form any words Charlie dropped a large rock on his big toe. Distracted by his howl of pain Hope fell silent. Charlie was hopping around on one foot. Poppy could quite cheerfully have dropped the biggest rock she could lift onto the other one.

"You were saying?" she said to Hope, trying her best to ignore her brother.

But Hope had wiped away her tears and her face was giving nothing away. Poppy knew she had missed her chance. The shutters had come down again and there was no way Hope was going to tell her what was wrong.

CHAPTER 17

Cloud's third X-ray after two months of box rest finally brought some good news.

"He looks a different pony, Poppy. You're doing a brilliant job," said the vet, casting an eye over the Connemara. It was true. Cloud's ribs had all but disappeared and the hollows in his flanks had filled out. Although he kept half an eye on Chester, who loved coming along to keep him company, he looked around with interest at the row of kennels and didn't flinch when the vet X-rayed his foot. Poppy felt immeasurably proud of him.

The hairline crack along his pedal bone was still visible – but only just.

"Another three or four weeks in his stable and I think we're there," said the vet, to Poppy's delight. "How's he coping with box rest?"

"He's bored out of his mind," admitted Poppy. "I

spend as long as possible with him but I'm at school most of the time. He has Chester for company but hates it when Chester's in the paddock and he's left behind in the stable."

"Try putting a carrot or apple on a string and hanging it from the roof. It'll give him something to nibble on. Or hide some Polos in his hay. Some people put shatterproof mirrors up in the stable so horses on box rest have something to look at. It sounds silly but it might do the trick. But the good news is I don't think he'll be stuck in there for too much longer."

When Poppy and Hope arrived at Redhall Manor for their lesson later that week Bella had some exciting news.

"You've both been doing so well with your flatwork that I thought we might try a bit of jumping. We'll start very slowly and see how it goes."

Poppy flew into the tack room, nearing colliding with Sam, who was on his way out with Buster's tack.

"Sorry!" Poppy said breathlessly. "I didn't see you."

"You don't say," he replied with a grin. For a moment Poppy forgot why she was there and gazed around blankly.

"Rosie's tack?" asked Sam helpfully. "It's at the end on the left, where it always is."

"Yes, alright thanks. No-one likes a smart Alec," she muttered, brushing past him, her face an unflattering shade of puce. Honestly, why were boys so annoying?

Bella was waiting next to three evenly-spaced red and white painted poles in the centre of the indoor school as Poppy and Hope rode in on Rosie and Buster.

"First we need to shorten your stirrups a couple of notches. Then we're going to start with some trotting poles," she said. "Trotting over these will help you learn to keep a well-balanced position that will stand you in good stead when you learn to jump. Buster's a bit lazy so you're going to need a lot of impulsion, Hope. But Rosie loves jumping, Poppy. Your problem will be holding her back."

After half an hour Bella, satisfied with their positions, put a low cross pole at the end. Poppy went first. Used to Flynn's lackadaisical approach to jumping she was unseated when Rosie flew over with a foot to spare.

"You're hanging onto the reins, Poppy. Your balance needs to come from your legs and your seat. Keep a good contact with Rosie but don't be heavy-handed."

"Sorry," mouthed Poppy, as she struggled to right herself and ease Rosie back into a balanced trot.

Hope proved a natural and was soon popping Buster over cross poles and cavalettis as though she'd been jumping for years. But Poppy struggled and by the end of the lesson her back ached and her arms felt as though they'd been pulled out of their sockets. Her face was the picture of dejection when she dismounted.

"Chin up, Poppy. I'm sure you'll get there in the end," boomed Bella from the other side of the yard. It wasn't exactly a vote of confidence, Poppy thought miserably. Sam was filling water buckets from the tap outside Rosie's stable and she felt her face grow hot. Trust him to have heard how useless she was.

Poppy didn't see his sympathetic smile as she passed – she was too busy looking at her feet. She untacked Rosie as slowly as she could and by the time she let herself out of the mare's stable Sam was thankfully nowhere to be seen.

She fared no better the following week. She was unseated every time Rosie jumped. The harder she tried not to lose her balance the more she tense she became and the more Rosie acted up.

"You're leaning too far forwards," shouted Bella. "Push your weight down into your heels so your lower legs don't tip back when Rosie jumps." But Poppy's back felt wooden and any connection she'd had with the roan mare during flatwork was long forgotten.

"Poppy, watch the way Hope stays balanced and keeps her hands steady as Buster approaches the jump. See how supple she is. She is going with the pony, not working against him. Don't worry if you can't anticipate where Rosie is going to take off, that'll come with practice. At this stage I just want you to relax and go with her. Enjoy it!" Bella commanded.

Poppy sat deep in the saddle and squeezed Rosie

into a canter. She was determined to show Bella that she was as good as Hope. As they approached the cavaletti she remembered not to hang onto Rosie's reins. But the sudden dropped contact in the last stride before the jump confounded the mare, who sloped her shoulders and stopped dead in her tracks. Poppy, on the other hand, flew over the jump and landed in a twisted heap on the floor. The impact knocked the wind out of her and for a few long moments she lay in a ball struggling for breath as Rosie careered delightedly around, throwing in a couple of bucks for good measure.

Caroline, watching the lesson from the small spectators' area, cried out in alarm and ran over to her stepdaughter, who was lying motionless on the ground. By the time she reached her Poppy's diaphragm had stopped going into spasm and she'd managed to gulp a few lungfuls of air.

"Only winded," she groaned, as Caroline held out a hand and pulled her to her feet. Sam appeared from nowhere and called softly to Rosie, who slowed to a stop and stood meekly for him. He led the mare to Poppy and held out her reins.

"It's always best to get straight back on," he advised.

Poppy dusted down her jodhpurs and grabbed the reins. "I do know that," she said ungraciously, putting her foot in the stirrup. Unfortunately as she sprang onto Rosie's back the mare's saddle slipped and, with a howl of frustration, she ended up on the floor again, her backside bruised and her pride well and truly dented.

CHAPTER 18

By the next morning Poppy was beginning to see the funny side of it all and had Scarlett in stitches on the school bus as she described her riding lesson from hell.

"Honestly, Scar, I couldn't have been any worse if I'd tried. I was *terrible*," she wailed.

"Wish I'd been there to see it," Scarlett giggled.

"I'm glad you weren't," said Poppy fervently. She paused. "I suppose what I'm most fed up about is that Hope is a natural. She just seems to get it."

"You'll get it too, don't worry," consoled Scarlett. "Forget about Rosie and jumping for a while. Why don't we take Blaze and Flynn up onto the moor for a picnic tomorrow? It'll be fun."

They set off just after ten, saddle bags filled with sandwiches, sausages rolls and Pat's homemade flapjacks. The sun shone weakly in a cloud-studded sky the colour of faded denim. Black-faced sheep skittered out of their way as they skirted the Riverdale tor and headed deep onto the moor. Flynn felt round and reassuringly solid after Rosie and Poppy felt herself relax.

"Why do I let myself get so uptight?" she asked Scarlett when they finally stopped for lunch beside a narrow stream.

"You're a perfectionist," answered Scarlett, passing Poppy a ham sandwich. "The trouble is, if you set your standards too high you're setting yourself up for a fall. In this case both metaphorically and literally," she giggled.

"Ha ha, very funny. I just want to be the best I can be for Cloud. Caitlyn was such a good rider I'm bound to be a disappointment to him," Poppy replied.

Scarlett was quiet for a moment. She wished Poppy could see what everyone else could – that she was kind, loyal and brave. "You mustn't compare yourself to other people, Poppy. If you want to be a better rider then do it for yourself, because it'll make you happier, not because you want to be better than Caitlyn or Hope."

"Maybe," said Poppy, unconvinced.

"I mean it. Everyone's different. You, for example, are rubbish at cooking, whereas I am a brilliant cake baker and probably should audition for the next series of the Great British Bake Off."

"Hey, that's a bit harsh! You were the one who

used plain flour remember," Poppy grinned. But she thought about what Scarlett had said as they rode home. Perhaps her friend was right. Maybe she shouldn't be so hard on herself.

They were ten minutes early for their next lesson at Redhall Manor and while Caroline and Hope plied Buster with Polos Poppy went off in search of Bella. She started with the tack room but that was empty, so she crossed the yard to the indoor school. The doors were closed which suggested Bella was giving a lesson. Poppy let herself into the spectators' area and sat down to watch.

The indoor school had been transformed into a mini Hickstead with a course of brightly-painted show jumps. A mixture of uprights, spreads, a double and a wall were all at least 100cm high and to Poppy looked enormous. Bella stood in the middle as a boy on a black pony cantered around the edge.

"Right, assume you've had a clear round and have made it into the jump off," boomed Bella. "Let's see how fast she can fly."

The pair approached the first jump, a rustic oxer. The pony's ears were pricked and the boy sat quietly as they cantered up to the jump, his hands light and his shoulders straight. It was only after they had cleared it with centimetres to spare that Poppy realised the boy was Sam, riding his Connemara mare, Star. She watched as they flew over a gate and swung around to jump the double. Sam turned the mare on a sixpence and she soared over a wall before turning to another oxer which they also cleared with ease. Sam whooped and lent down to pat the mare's neck as she slowed to a walk.

"Nice job, Sam. If you can do that at the weekend you'll make mincemeat of the competition," said Bella. As she strode over to her grandson she saw Poppy watching. "We're holding an affiliated jumping show here on Saturday," she explained. "People are coming from across the west of Devon to compete. Obviously as a riding instructor I should tell you that it's the taking part not the winning that matters. But it will be good if Sam can win a couple of ribbons for Redhall. It's a great advertisement for the riding school."

"No pressure then Gran," grinned Sam, as he dismounted. He ran up the stirrup leathers and loosened Star's girth a couple of notches. "Although she's jumping out of her skin at the moment."

Poppy, who had been wondering ruefully if she'd ever reach Sam's standard of riding, remembered Scarlett's words. Everyone was different. Some people were excellent at jumping, others were better at baking cakes. She, on the other hand, was pretty damn good at falling off. She smiled to herself and said graciously, "Lovely round. Good luck for Saturday."

"Thanks. Maybe you'll come along to watch?"

"'Er, not sure. I'll have to ask Caroline. Shall I go and tack up Rosie?" she asked Bella.

"Yes please, Poppy. I'm going to put these fences right down to about a foot and we'll see how you both get on jumping a course shall we?"

Poppy made a conscious decision not to try too hard. She pretended that Rosie was solid, dependable Flynn and that they were jumping cavaletti in the field at Ashworthy with no-one watching them but a few sheep. The New Forest mare sensed that her rider was more relaxed and settled to the task without a quibble. Soon they were popping over the fences as easily as Hope and Buster. Poppy still found it hard to judge Rosie's strides but Bella reminded her that it would come with practice. By the end of the lesson she felt immensely cheered. Perhaps she would be able to master this jumping lark one day after all.

Caroline was happy to drive them all to Redhall Manor for the horse show. Scarlett had already agreed to go and Poppy couldn't wait to tell Hope. She cycled to Flint Cottage, leant her bike against the rickety fence at the front of the house and rang the bell. Hope answered the door and smiled when she saw Poppy on the doorstep.

"Is your mum out?" asked Poppy hopefully

"No, she's upstairs re-decorating her bedroom. She's bought some new furniture which is due to arrive next week. She wanted to get the room painted and the new carpet in before it arrives."

"Is she going to decorate your room, too?" said Poppy, picturing the scuffed magnolia walls and chipped melamine furniture in Hope's cheerless bedroom.

"Oh, I don't think so. She hasn't mentioned it."

What a surprise, thought Poppy.

"Anyway, the reason I came over is that Scarlett and I are going to Redhall Manor this afternoon to watch the jumping and we wondered if you'd like to come?"

"I'd love to. But I'd better ask Mum. Won't be a minute."

Poppy waited awkwardly while Hope disappeared upstairs. She picked up a handful of letters from the doormat. Several were addressed to the Hope for Hope Appeal c/o Flint Cottage. A brown envelope at the bottom of the pile was for a Mrs M. Turner.

Hope bounded down the stairs, grinning. "Mum says yes as long as Caroline doesn't mind picking me up and dropping me off."

"No problem," said Poppy, handing Hope the letters. "Looks like that one's for the old lady who used to live here. I thought she died ages ago," she observed.

The grin slid from Hope's face. She grabbed the envelopes and dropped them on the kitchen table as if they were hot to the touch.

"You alright?" Poppy asked, surprised at Hope's sudden change of mood.

"Of course! Why wouldn't I be?"

"Just asking. Anyway I promised I wouldn't be long. I'd better go. We'll pick you up at two."

CHAPTER 19

Poppy hadn't realised the size of the show until they drove up to the entrance of Redhall Manor and saw the number of horse lorries and trailers parked on the hardstanding next to the main yard. While Caroline found a place to park the girls gawped at the goings-on around them. Everywhere they looked there was something to see. A girl with a long blonde plait down her back was bending down to undo her chestnut pony's travel boots. A boy dressed in white breeches and a black jacket was leading a strikingly handsome skewbald cob down the ramp of a trailer. Elsewhere people were re-plaiting manes, tying stocks, grooming and tacking up.

"This brings it all back," said Caroline, who had finally found a space to park. "I used to love going to shows with Hamilton. We never went to one quite this big though."

As they headed towards the indoor school a girl about their age rode past them, scowling. She hauled her grey pony to a halt outside a smart sky blue lorry, dismounted and flung the pony's reins at a harassed-looking woman who was grooming a dark bay mare tied to the side of the lorry. "He totally misjudged his stride in the double and knocked down the spread," the girl announced in a clipped voice.

"Never mind," soothed the woman. "Let's hope Barley can do better."

"I sincerely hope so. Where is he?"

"In the back of the box. I've tacked him up so he's ready to go."

Scarlett nudged Poppy. "That's Georgia Canning. She went to my old school until her parents came into money and moved her to Beresford House." Seeing Poppy and Hope's blank faces Scarlett explained, "It's this really posh girls' boarding school on the other side of Okehampton."

The friends watched Georgia stomp up the ramp of the deluxe horse lorry and appear two minutes later dragging a flashy palomino behind her.

"Mum!" she yelled. The woman tied the grey pony next to the bay mare, took the palomino's reins and gave her daughter a leg up. Georgia turned the pony and clattered off towards the outdoor ménage where riders were warming up over a couple of jumps.

"Good luck, Georgie," the woman called to her daughter's retreating back. But her words were carried away with the wind. When she turned back to the bay mare her face was resigned.

Scarlett raised her eyebrows at Poppy, Hope and Caroline. Once they were out of earshot she said, "Georgia's mum used to work in a supermarket and her dad was a builder. They lived in a three bedroomed semi and had a clapped out old hatchback. Now they live in this enormous mansion, her dad drives around in a Bentley and her mum has a Range Rover."

Hope's eyes widened. "Did they win the football pools or something?"

"Georgia's parents always claimed they inherited the money but Mum is convinced it was a lottery win. And a big one at that. Georgia used to beg me to let her have a ride on Blaze. Now she has a string of about five jumping ponies and her own personal riding instructor. Imagine that!"

"Were you friends at school then?" Poppy asked, surprised. She couldn't imagine Scarlett befriending the haughty Georgia Canning.

"Not really. She was in the year above me. But our mums were friendly. I think they used to take us to the same toddler group. You know what it's like around here, Poppy. Everyone knows each other," Scarlett grimaced. Sometimes she found village life suffocating and longed to live in a place where no-one knew her name, let alone remembered her wearing a false beard to play the part of Joseph in the school nativity when she was five. "Shall we go and watch them warming up before we go inside?"

They leant on the post and rail fence of the outdoor ménage. Poppy studied Georgia's face as she trotted the palomino around the ring. She had china blue eyes and hair as black as molasses. With her high cheekbones and flawless English rose complexion she could have been a child model if it hadn't been for an imperfection Poppy only noticed when she cantered past. In profile Georgia had a hooked Roman nose that was at odds with her otherwise perfect features. It lent her face a superior expression that bordered on arrogance. She turned the pony towards a spread and jumped it easily, the palomino's tail swishing as it landed.

"She's a really good rider," Poppy observed.

"We all would be if we had our own riding instructor and the best ponies money could buy. I'm going to outgrow Blaze any minute now and there's no way Mum and Dad can afford to buy me one new pony, let alone five. Not with the way things are with the farm at the moment. It's alright for some," Scarlett said gloomily as Georgia cantered past.

"Cheer up," said Poppy, linking arms with her friend. "I think you're a brilliant rider, much better than Georgia Canning. Come on, let's go and watch the jumping."

They found their seats in the spectators' area and settled down to watch a BSJA affiliated open class for ponies up to 148cm.

"That's 14.2hh to you," Poppy told Caroline kindly.

"They're jumping a 100cm course, which is three feet three inches high if you were born in the Dark Ages."

"Yes, thank you for that Poppy," her stepmum replied drily. "I'm not that old, you know. It's just that when it comes to horses I'm conditioned to think in hands, feet and inches." They watched a girl on a blue roan demolish the wall, sending bricks flying. "I wonder how many clear rounds there have been."

As she spoke the girl on the roan pony exited in tears and Georgia Canning entered the ring, her back ramrod straight and her jaw set. Her pony looked balanced and alert.

"She looks as though she means business," Poppy said. She was right. The pair executed a textbook clear round, the palomino sailing over the jumps with ease. There was a faint ripple of applause and Georgia gave a superior smile. But she didn't pat her pony, Poppy noticed.

"Georgia's mum paid over ten thousand pounds for that pony apparently," said Scarlett. "He a JA, of course."

"What does that mean?" asked Hope, who had been watching the round mesmerised.

"That he's won more than £700 in prize money. He's her top jumping pony. She competes all over the South West on him."

"Look, Sam's next," said Caroline.

"Who's Sam?" asked Scarlett.

"He's Bella Thompson's grandson and he works at Redhall Manor. We see him when we have our lessons every Thursday. His pony's a Connemara like Cloud, but she's a mare and she's called Star," said Hope, pleased to be able to put Scarlett in the picture for a change.

"I've heard all about Bella, Rosie and Buster. You didn't mention Sam though, Poppy," said Scarlett, an amused expression on her face.

"Oh, didn't I?" Poppy asked airily. "Yes, anyway, that's him."

Sam, who had been scanning the spectators as he cantered past, saw where they were sitting and waved. Star's black coat gleamed. Her mane and tail were plaited and Sam had brushed a checkerboard quarter mark on her rump. She looked stunning. The bell went, Sam ran his hand down Star's neck and cantered towards the first jump, a blue and white painted spread.

Poppy was so engrossed watching Sam and Star fly round the course that she didn't notice Bella sit down next to them and jumped when Bella boomed, "Good job, Sam!" as her grandson cleared the last fence with inches to spare. Poppy grimaced at Bella's habit of talking at the same volume regardless of whether you were at the other end of the indoor school or sitting right next to her.

"That's six clear rounds, so he'll get a ribbon whatever," she told them with satisfaction. "With any luck he'll show that Canning girl a thing or two in the jump-off. I used to teach her, you know. Then she decided she wanted some fancy trainer from I don't know where and left Redhall."

The stewards came in and raised some fences for the shortened jump-off course. A boy on a fleabitten grey was first to jump. The pony was totally over-excited and crabbed into the ring sideways. The bell went and the boy gave the pony his head. He raced towards the blue and white spread and took off far too early, jumping flat and knocking a pole out with his back legs. The boy struggled to regain control and notched up a cricket score by the time he finished the round.

The next rider fared no better. Attempting to turn too tightly into the gate the pony lost its impulsion and refused. The third rider, a girl on a diminutive Exmoor with characteristic mealy markings around its eyes and muzzle, jumped clear, to a loud round of applause, but at well over a minute her time was slow. The fourth rider was eliminated after taking the wrong course and then it was the turn of Georgia Canning, who cantered in on her flashy palomino as if she owned Redhall Manor.

"She's fast," said Poppy, as Georgia and her pony galloped around the course. They were jumping clear until the last jump, a double. The palomino flew over the upright but flattened over the spread, giving the pole a hefty clout. It rattled in the cup and Poppy saw Georgia glance over her shoulder, her face like thunder. But luck was on her side. The pole didn't fall and the pair notched up their second clear round in a time of fifty six seconds.

"Sam and Star have their work cut out to beat that," Caroline said.

"The fastest horses don't necessarily win," Bella told her. "In a jump-off it's often the balanced, accurate riders who take the shortest route who clinch it. And jump-offs are Star's speciality. She loves them."

Sam trotted into the ring. He halted, nodded to the judge and squeezed Star into a canter. The black mare's ears were pricked as she approached the first jump. Poppy realised she was holding her breath. Sam might be irritating but Poppy had taken an instant dislike to the spoilt, sneering Georgia Canning. She knew whose side she was on, no question.

Sam and Star's round was a lesson in accomplished horsemanship. He sat quietly, perfectly balanced as the pony soared over the fences. They turned inside the wall, saving crucial seconds, but still managed to leap over the gate almost from a standstill. Poppy checked the clock. Forty five seconds with only the double to go. They cleared the first part but as Star took off for the second part of the combination Poppy gasped – one of the cups was dangling precariously where it had been knocked by Georgia Canning's palomino, leaving the back pole hanging on a thread. Star cleared the pole by an inch but the impact of her landing was enough to dislodge it and it crashed to the ground as the mare crossed the finish line in just fifty one seconds. Sam looked back ruefully, wrapped his arms around his pony's neck and cantered out of the ring.

"That's not fair!" cried Hope, who had been sitting on the edge of her seat, chewing her nails. "Star didn't even touch the pole. It was Georgia who knocked it."

"That's the luck of the draw, I'm afraid," said Bella. "I should have asked the stewards to check the fence. Still, he's got third place. And the satisfaction of knowing that he knocked five seconds off the Canning girl's time. On any other day he would have been first."

CHAPTER 20

Georgia Canning accepted her small silver cup with a supercilious smile and kicked her palomino into a canter to lead the lap of honour. But the biggest cheer went to Sam and Star as they cantered past the spectators.

"That's because everyone knows he should have won," said Hope with feeling.

When they joined Sam outside the indoor school he was as sanguine as his grandmother. "It's just one of those things. Luck'll be on my side next time," he assured Hope.

Scarlett dug Poppy in the ribs. "Aren't you going to introduce us then?"

Poppy sighed. "Scarlett, this is Sam. Sam is Bella's grandson and works at Redhall. Sam, this is my best friend Scarlett. She talks a lot."

"Charming," said Scarlett. "Hello Sam. I'd love to

say I've heard all about you but it wouldn't be true. Anyway I thought you and Star were brilliant and -".

Before Scarlett could finish Georgia rode up. "Bad luck, Sam. It really wasn't your day, was it? Only managed to scrape a third on home turf? Not much of an advert for Redhall, is it?" she taunted.

Scarlett's auburn eyebrows shot up so high they almost touched her hairline and Poppy stared at Georgia in stunned silence, astonished at her audacity. Only Sam seemed unperturbed.

"Oh well, you can't win 'em all. Star was the fastest on the day, and I'm happy with that," he said, patting his mare's coal-black neck and smiling at the three girls.

"Brought your fan club today, I see. Wait a minute, don't I know you?" she said to Scarlett.

"Never seen you before in my life," said Scarlett, deadpan. Georgia frowned and was about to speak when her palomino shied at a passing lorry. She cursed under her breath, gathered her reins and turned her attention to Sam again.

"Our offer still stands, you know."

"The answer's no. Again," he told Georgia. His hand was clenched tightly around Star's reins and a muscle twitched in his jaw.

"You won't get a better offer," she insisted.

"She's not for sale. And even if she was I wouldn't sell her to you if you were the last person on earth, Georgia Canning. Come on girl, let's get you back to your stable," he told Star. He held up his hand in a mock salute to Poppy, Scarlett and Hope and turned his mare towards the yard. Georgia watched them go, her expression stony.

A paint-splattered Shelley opened the door of Flint Cottage when they dropped Hope off on their way home.

"Are you rushing off?" she asked Caroline. Poppy crossed her fingers inside her jacket pocket hoping Caroline would say no.

"Actually I could murder a cup of tea. But we can't stay too long. I promised I'd get Scarlett back before six," she said.

They piled into the lounge. Scarlett had never been inside Flint Cottage and she looked around avidly. Her eyes widened when she noticed the flat screen television.

"Blimey Hope, your TV's as big as a cinema screen. It must have cost a fortune."

"What? Oh, it's ex-display or something," she muttered, sitting next to Poppy and chewing the nail of her index finger.

Shelley appeared from the kitchen carrying a teapot and mugs on an old metal tray. She swept a tabloid newspaper, a holiday brochure and some clothing catalogues off the coffee table and kicked them under the sofa before placing the tray on the table. "Try not to knock it flying this time, you clumsy oaf," she told Hope coldly.

"So, did you enjoy your first horse show, Hope?"

Caroline asked.

Hope hadn't stopped talking about the show on the way home. As she'd chattered about the ponies they'd seen and the riders they'd met even Scarlett had struggled to get a word in edgeways, and that didn't happen very often. But suddenly Hope was monosyllabic.

"It was OK, thanks," she said, her knuckles white as she clasped her mug of tea.

"She had a great time," Scarlett told Shelley. "Though we were all fed up when Georgia Canning won the open jumping. But it's easy to be the best if you throw enough money at it. Mum reckons they won the lottery a few years back, though no-one knows for sure. They're really cagey about it. But it must have been a massive win."

Shelley's eyes lit up. "What makes you think that?"

"They live in a huge mansion, drive flash cars and own loads of ponies. Georgia's an only child and she's spoilt rotten. The pony she won the open jumping on cost ten thousand pounds," Scarlett continued.

"Ten grand? For one pony? You're kidding, right?" Shelley was incredulous.

"That's a drop in the ocean for the Cannings. Apparently their house is absolutely rammed full of antiques and works of art."

"Have you been to their house? Where is it?"

"It's called Claydon Manor and it's on the outskirts of Tavistock. You know the kind of place. Wrought iron automatic gates, a long, sweeping drive and security cameras everywhere. I think they even have guard dogs. I suppose they're worried about being burgled."

"Honestly, it makes me sick. Here I am, a single mum with next to nothing, doing everything I can to send my poor daughter to America for life-saving cancer treatment when people like that have so much money they could write a cheque for the whole trip tomorrow if they wanted to," said Shelley.

Hope stood up abruptly, muttered something about needing the bathroom and disappeared out of the room. Caroline looked at her watch, taken aback by the seething resentment in Shelley's voice.

"Heavens, it's ten to six. We'd better make a move."

Poppy stared at her reflection in the car window on the way home, half-listening to Caroline and Scarlett as they talked about Christmas while her mind drifted over the events of the day. She wondered what Georgia Canning, the girl who had everything, would be given for Christmas. Not Star, that was for sure. Apparently there were some things money couldn't buy after all. Poppy pictured Shelley's face, calculating and covetous. Scarlett had certainly touched a nerve when she'd described the Cannings' fortune. Yet for someone who was always pleading poverty Shelley always seemed to be spending money – on herself at least. And finally, Poppy thought about Hope. All she must want for Christmas was a chance to get better. But would she be given that chance?

CHAPTER 21

Poppy couldn't shake a growing sense of unease that behind the shabby front door of Flint Cottage all was not as it should be. On the car journeys to Redhall Manor Hope opened up like a flower, talking about Buster and his idiosyncrasies and quizzing Poppy about Cloud and Chester. The minute they dropped her home she clammed up. Her face was guarded. Wary, even. The day they'd walked to the top of the Riverdale tor Poppy knew that Hope was a heartbeat away from confiding in her. But since then Hope changed the subject every time Poppy tried to raise it and she was no nearer to gleaning the truth.

One night, as she sat at the kitchen table struggling with her maths homework while Caroline tested Charlie on his spellings, a theory began to take shape. It was formed by a chance remark from Charlie, who hated homework more than he hated Brussels sprouts. And that was saying something.

"I bet Hope never has homework," the six-year-old grumbled. "She doesn't even go to school. I thought everyone had to go to school. So how come Hope doesn't?"

"You know why, Charlie. It's because she's got cancer. Her mum is giving her lessons at home because she has a weak immune system," Caroline reminded him.

"She looks pretty healthy to me," he said.

"Charlie!" Caroline admonished. "She's in remission, that's all. She's still a very sick little girl."

"Well, I'd like to be in remission if it meant I didn't have to do stupid spellings," he announced, flinging down his pencil in disgust. "It's not fair."

"Come on now, there's no need to throw a strop. Homework is really important, isn't it Poppy?" Caroline looked to her stepdaughter for support, but Poppy's thoughts were far away in Flint Cottage. Random images that had seemed unrelated were gradually connecting in her mind.

"Poppy?" Caroline repeated.

"Sorry, I was miles away. Yes, Charlie, homework is really important. Speaking of which, I need the laptop to look up something for science. Is it OK to take it up to my room?"

Poppy spent the next hour on the internet hopping from one website to another, frowning to herself as pieces of the puzzle gradually fell into place. True, she had made a few assumptions and a lot of her 'evidence' was conjecture. But there were far too many coincidences for her liking. Just as Poppy knew it would never hold up in a court of law, she was also certain she was right.

When she woke the next morning she had come to a decision.

"I'll be on the late bus tonight. I want to pop in and see Tory," she said over breakfast.

"No problem. I'll see to Chester and Cloud so there's no rush. Give her our love." Caroline's blonde head was bent over the dishwasher and her voice was muffled. She and Charlie were so lucky, Poppy thought. Caroline was such a kind, easy-going person. Perhaps her only fault was that sometimes she only saw the good in people. When her stepmum straightened up Poppy crossed the kitchen and gave her a quick hug.

"Hey, what's that for sweetheart? Everything OK?"

"Yes," Poppy brushed her fringe out of her eyes. "I'm just glad you're you, that's all."

"Well, I'm glad you're you, too, angel. And I'm glad Charlie is Charlie. Most of the time anyway," she laughed. "Right, we'd better get ourselves into gear otherwise you'll both be late for school."

Poppy kept her head down as she arrived at the block of sheltered flats in Tavistock. She was hoping to avoid the warden, an overbearing woman called Mrs Parker, who usually bent her ear for ten minutes berating the youth of today. But luck was on her side and there was no sign of the old battleaxe. Poppy sighed with relief as she scooted down the dimly-lit corridor, stopped outside Tory's front door and knocked. Tory's lined face creased into a smile when she saw Poppy.

"Hello pet, how lovely to see you. Come in. I'll put the kettle on." Tory reached down for Poppy's rucksack. "Lummy, what've you got in there – bricks? It's a wonder you haven't given yourself a hernia carting that around all day."

"You get used to it after a while. And who on earth is Lummy?" said Poppy, taking the bag from Tory and hefting it over her shoulder.

"Oh, it's an expression my old mum used to use. I don't suppose anyone says it any more. One sugar, isn't it? Or would you prefer a hot chocolate? I've plenty of milk."

"Hot chocolate please, Tory." Poppy shrugged off her coat and blazer and sat down in the stiflingly hot sitting room while Tory pottered about in the kitchen. Poppy automatically reached for the framed photograph of Caitlyn and Cloud, taken at the Brambleton Horse Show more than five years before. Although she had consigned it to memory long ago she still scrutinised the photo every time she visited. It fed her obsessive need to find out everything she could about Caitlyn. Cloud's mane was plaited and his dappled grey coat gleamed. He looked muscled and fit, every inch the champion pony as the red rosette was hooked onto his browband. Caitlyn's black show jacket matched her polished black leather riding boots and her white breeches were spotless. She was grinning into the camera, her joy at winning the open jumping class pure and unadulterated. No-one looking at the golden pair could have predicted that a few months later Caitlyn would be dead and Cloud would be a broken shadow of himself, running wild on the moor with the Dartmoor ponies. Poppy knew it was crazy to be jealous of a dead girl. She placed the photo carefully back on Tory's oak side table and remembered why she had come.

"So how are you all? How are Cloud and Chester?" said the old woman as she settled herself in the other armchair.

"They're both fine. Cloud's still putting on weight and is much less nervy around people, especially Caroline. He'll even let her pick up his feet now. Dad's in Syria at the moment."

"I know, pet. I saw him on the late news last night."

Poppy took a deep breath. "Tory, what would you do if you thought someone you knew had committed a crime?"

The old woman paused before she replied, her eyebrows knotted in concern.

"What kind of crime, Poppy?"

"I'm sorry, I can't tell you at the moment. But it's not murder or anything," she added quickly.

"Well, I suppose I would tackle the person I thought was responsible and give them the chance to own up. And if they weren't prepared to do that I would tell the police myself. I don't think I could turn a blind eye. It wouldn't be right."

"Mm. That's what I thought, too. I just wanted to run it past someone first. Thanks Tory."

"You're not in any trouble are you?" asked her old friend.

"It's nothing to do with me. I've just discovered something that needs to be put right. I'll tell you as soon as I can." Poppy was silent until a thought occurred to her. "Does George Blackstone have any children?"

"Goodness me, no. Can you imagine anyone wanting to marry him?" Tory chuckled. "He had a brother, Cyril, but he died thirty odd years ago. His widow was left to bring up their daughter all on her own."

"Does she live in Waterby?"

"No, she moved away with the little one soon after Cyril died and hasn't been back since."

"Can you remember what the daughter was called?"

"It was a long time ago. I'm afraid my memory isn't what it was. I can hardly remember what I had for breakfast these days." As the smell of toast constantly pervaded Tory's small flat Poppy thought she could probably hazard a guess, but kept the thought to herself. Tory, meanwhile, was adding two and two together and getting pretty close to the mark.

"Is this anything to do with the secret you've

uncovered," she asked, her faded blue eyes suddenly flint sharp.

Poppy realised that she should have been more subtle in her line of questioning. "I just wondered, that's all." As she looked around for inspiration her eyes fell on the clock on Tory's mantelpiece.

"Crikey, is that the time? I'd better go or I'll miss the bus."

CHAPTER 22

For the next few weeks Poppy was swept up in the build up to Christmas. During their weekly riding lessons she watched Hope like a hawk. The Tavistock Herald continued to print updates on the Hope for Hope Appeal as villagers organised quiz nights, boot fairs and even a sponsored walk to raise money to send Hope to America. Poppy knew she would have to tackle her friend soon, but the days were so packed with school carol concerts, end of term productions and Christmas shopping expeditions that she didn't have time to stop and think.

The weekend before Christmas Caroline drove them to Bromley to stay with her sister Lizzie. Scarlett had offered to look after Cloud and Chester while they were away and was patiently responding to the text messages Poppy was sending hourly to check all was well.

On Saturday evening, after a frenetic trip into London to see the Christmas lights, Poppy sat curled up on the sofa in Lizzie's chaotic kitchen watching the two sisters prepare dinner. Charlie was on the rug by her feet playing with an old box of Lego that Lizzie had unearthed in the loft. Poppy was exhausted. She'd felt strangely out of place as they'd jostled with hordes of Christmas shoppers in Oxford Street. They'd only moved from Twickenham to Devon six months earlier but she already felt like a country mouse visiting her cousins in the city. She wasn't used to seeing so many people in one place at one time. She also missed Cloud with an ache that refused to go away. After texting Scarlett yet again she picked up a crumpled copy of the local paper from the arm of the sofa and began flicking through it. As she scanned story after story of police incidents, council intrigue and court cases she had a flash of inspiration.

"Auntie Lizzie, can I borrow your computer for a minute? I want to Skype Scarlett, just to check how things are at home."

Lizzie stopped chopping vegetables. "Of course you can, darling. You know where it is, don't you?"

Poppy nodded and made her way to the cellar, which had been converted into a den. She switched on the computer and within a couple of minutes the freckled face of her best friend was grinning at her as if she was in the same room, not two hundred and fifty miles away on the edge of Dartmoor.

"How's London? Did you get a chance to go to Harrods or Hamleys? What were the Christmas lights like? I bet they were a million times better than the ones at home. Honestly, Poppy, sometimes I feel like I live in the back of beyond."

"You are funny, Scar. I can't wait to get home. London is so *busy*. Anyway, how are Cloud and Chester?"

"They're fine. We've just been over to check. Cloud was lying down in his stable and Chester was standing watching over him. They're so sweet together."

"I know. It's almost as if Chester is Cloud's guardian angel. I miss them so much."

"You're back tomorrow evening, aren't you? Only one more sleep," teased Scarlett.

"Thank goodness. Have you seen Hope?" Poppy asked.

"No. We spent yesterday in Plymouth finishing off the Christmas shopping and drove over to see Great Aunt Lucy today."

"Where does she live?" asked Poppy, homesick for Devon.

"Near Holsworthy. She's my dad's spinster auntie and used to be the head teacher of an all-girls boarding school. She's totally terrifying. But she makes a lovely fruit cake."

"While we're on the subject of old ladies, what was the name of the woman who lived at Flint Cottage before Hope and Shelley?"

"Mrs Deakins. She died ages ago."

"So why would someone be sending letters to Flint Cottage addressed to a Mrs M. Turner?"

"Search me."

"Scar, I've been thinking about Hope and her mum, about the appeal and everything."

"And?"

Scarlett listened intently as Poppy voiced her suspicions. Even to her own ears they sounded implausible. And yet…

"Are you sure?" Scarlett was scandalised.

"Not one hundred per cent," Poppy admitted. "Maybe my imagination's running away with me. But there are too many coincidences. I just need to find a way of proving I'm right. What would the name Shelley be short for?"

"Michelle?" Scarlett hazarded.

"That's what I thought. Look, there's something I want to try. In the meantime promise me you'll keep it to yourself? It would be awful if I was wrong."

"Of course I promise, you twit. As long as you promise to keep me posted."

They ended the connection and Poppy sat twiddling a strand of hair that had come loose from her ponytail. She began typing furiously into a search engine and at last found a website that confirmed her suspicions. The reason for Hope's secrecy was there in black and white. But Poppy felt no sense of triumph. She switched off the computer with a heavy heart.

CHAPTER 23

Poppy carried the weight of her untold secret heavily until Monday morning, the first day of the Christmas holidays. After mucking out and feeding Cloud and Chester she ran virtually all the way to Ashworthy. By the time she reached Scarlett's back door she was panting heavily. Scarlett led her up to her bedroom, where Poppy collapsed on the floor in a sweaty heap.

"Well?" demanded Scarlett.

"I was right. Look, it's all here," said Poppy, waving a printout from Lizzie's computer in Scarlett's face. She grabbed it and Poppy watched her eyes widen as she started reading.

"Poor Hope," Scarlett whispered. "What are we going to do?"

"Nothing. At least not for a few days." Poppy had made the decision in the early hours. "Let's all enjoy

Christmas first. Then we can come up with a plan of action."

Mike McKeever's plane was due to land at Heathrow early on Christmas Eve and he'd promised to be home just after lunch. Poppy spent the morning sweeping out the tack room, wrestling with spider webs and re-arranging the grooming kit, tack, rugs and feed bins into some semblance of order before giving Caroline a hand indoors.

"Just as well your dad's back today," Caroline remarked as she and Poppy wrapped streaky bacon around cocktail sausages and rolled sage, onion and chestnut stuffing into balls. "Snow's forecast tonight."

"A white Christmas! Seriously?" said Charlie. "That would be epic!"

Poppy had purloined the McKeevers' old artificial tree for her bedroom and had adorned it with the leftover tinsel, baubles and homemade creations she had found at the bottom of their enormous cardboard box of Christmas decorations. Some, including the toilet roll fairy for the top of the tree, had been made when Poppy was at pre-school and her mum was still alive. Right at the bottom of the box were a couple of red felt stocking decorations that Poppy still remembered embellishing with buttons and ribbon. She pictured her four-year-old self, her brown hair falling forward and her tongue between her teeth as she concentrated on getting glue on the buttons and ribbons and not her fingers, her mum helping with the tricky bits. The memory made her smile.

Just after two o'clock she heard car doors slam and by the time she had run downstairs her dad was already in the hallway, hanging his jacket on the bottom of the bannister. Poppy flung her arms around him.

"Hello, my gorgeous girl. How's Cloud? Is his leg better yet?" he asked.

"You're hopeless, Dad. It's his foot, not his leg. And no, not yet. His next X-ray is due in a fortnight."

"Foot, leg, it's all the same to me. How are the riding lessons going?"

"Brilliant. We've moved on from flatwork to pole work and a bit of jumping now. I'm working on my contact and impulsion and getting Rosie into a nice outline."

Her dad ruffled her hair. "I've got absolutely no idea what you're talking about but it all sounds very impressive."

They spent the afternoon catching up and, after an early tea, settled down in front of the fire to watch a Christmas film.

"I love Christmas Eve better than Christmas Day, if I'm honest," said Caroline. "I remember when I was your age Poppy, I used to creep downstairs in the middle of the night to go and see Hamilton." Poppy pictured a young Caroline tiptoeing down the stairs to see the fleabitten grey pony she'd owned as a girl. "I'd read about this legend that claimed that animals were able to talk at the stroke of midnight on Christmas

Eve," her stepmum continued. "I tried it two years running but no luck. He was pleased to see me and I think I got a whicker but he never said a word. I gave up after that."

That night Poppy set the alarm on her mobile phone for a quarter to midnight, making sure it was on vibrate mode before shoving it under her pillow. When the pillow started shuddering a couple of hours later it took her several minutes to come to but when she did she dressed quickly. She tugged the duvet from her bed, dragging it silently behind her like a bride's train, down the stairs, through the hallway and into the kitchen. Stuck on the back door was a note, written in Caroline's familiar handwriting.

I thought you might be heading for the stables. Give Cloud and Chester my love and don't forget to tell me if the magic works for you!

Poppy was grinning as she pulled on her coat and wellies and let herself out of the back door.

It was a cloudy night and bitingly cold. She could almost taste the ice in the air. She lent on the stable door and peered in. It took a few moments for her eyes to adjust to the inky blackness inside but as she stared the outlines of Cloud and Chester slowly began to take shape. They were standing nose to tail, their heads drooping as they slept.

Poppy checked her watch. Ten to midnight. Almost Christmas. The day was always bittersweet. It was the day more than any other that she missed her mum. Poppy often wondered if the gash in her heart left by Isobel's death would ever fully heal. Her mum had adored Christmas and had always gone completely over the top, throwing decorations at their Twickenham home until it resembled Santa's grotto in Hamleys. She'd insisted on inviting more relatives than could comfortably squeeze into their terraced home, and the party usually lasted for several days. Caroline's approach was more measured. They'd still had a six foot tree in the bay window of their front room but until this year they had always spent the day itself at Lizzie's in Bromley.

Poppy gazed at Cloud, his face now so familiar to her that she could have drawn it from memory. Something cold landed on her nose, making her start. It was a flake of snow, sparkling in the beam cast by the security light over the stable door. She squinted into the dark. More flakes were coming, falling from the sky like tiny parachutes, dancing in the gusts. It was going to be a white Christmas. Charlie would be so excited. For the first time since Isobel's death, Poppy felt her mother's presence so keenly it was as if she was standing beside her, her arm wrapped around Poppy's shoulders.

She eased open the bolt on the door and crept into the stable. Cloud, who had only been dozing, woke and turned towards her. When he realised it was Poppy he gave the softest whicker. Chester jerked his head up, opened his liquid brown eyes and hee-hawed loudly.

"Shh! It's only me," whispered Poppy. "I wanted to

wish you both a happy Christmas." And see if you would talk to me at midnight, she thought, even though she knew it was as unlikely as finding snow in the Sahara. Chester shook his woolly head, dismissing such nonsense, walked over and started nibbling her pockets. Cloud gave her a friendly nudge.

"OK, OK, be patient," Poppy told them, fishing around for a packet of Polos. She gave them one each and popped a third into her mouth before settling in the corner of the stable, the duvet wrapped around her. As all three crunched companionably Poppy smiled contentedly. She checked her watch. A couple of minutes to go.

"If someone had told me a year ago that I'd be spending the next Christmas Eve with my own pony and donkey I'd have thought they were crackers," she said. Right now Dartmoor seemed light years away from leafy Twickenham. "I thought I was the unluckiest girl in the world when my mum died. I thought so for years. But not any more. It's like my luck changed the moment we moved to Riverdale. Perhaps there is magic here."

Cloud locked eyes with her and she crossed her fingers, willing him to speak. "It's midnight, Cloud. It's now or never," she whispered.

The stable was so quiet a field mouse could have dropped a miniature pin and no-one would have heard it fall. Poppy held her breath.

Cloud, her perfect pony, her beautiful boy, lifted his silver tail and broke wind noisily. The sound reverberated around the stable's four walls like a rumble of thunder. Poppy felt bubbles of laughter rising from deep inside her belly and was soon bent double, cackling like a hyena. "So much for Christmas Eve magic," she spluttered. "Wait until Caroline hears about this!"

CHAPTER 24

"Poppy! Wake up!" The command was whispered in her ear, dispatched on a wave of warm breath that tickled her earlobe. Poppy pulled the duvet over her face. "Go away. I'm asleep," she muttered, rolling over to face the wall. But Charlie was not deterred that easily. He tried a different tack.

"Poppy?" he wheedled through the duck down duvet. "Poppy, please wake up. It's Christmas! Santa's been. My stocking's full of presents!"

"What time is it?" she growled.

"I don't know. It's still dark outside but it must be nearly morning. I've been awake for *hours*."

Poppy turned over and grabbed her alarm clock. Twenty to five. Charlie had been given strict instructions the night before not to wake Caroline and their dad before half past six. Poppy sighed. "We've got ages before we can open any presents.

You must be freezing. Come on, hop into bed and I'll warm you up."

Charlie's feet were like blocks of ice. She shuddered as he wound them around her legs. He put his thumb in his mouth and mumbled, "Will you tell me a story while we wait?"

Poppy knew she had no chance of getting back to sleep. "Oh alright then, seeing as it's Christmas," she said. "What kind of story?"

"One about how Freddie and Cloud used to live together on the moor and how they became friends with the panther. Please," he added as an afterthought.

Poppy paused. She never minded talking about Cloud. "Once upon a time there was a beautiful Connemara pony called Cloud. His dappled grey coat was the colour of slate and snow and his mane and tail rippled like molten silver as he galloped across the moor. He was wild and untamed yet had the kindest, biggest heart. His best friend in all the world was a dog called Freddie, who was loyal and brave. Freddie was the best companion any pony could hope to have by their side. One day, as Cloud and Freddie walked together through the Riverdale wood -" As Poppy's story of adventure and derring-do unfolded she felt Charlie grow heavy beside her, his breathing slowing. She felt tiredness seep through her body and soon she, too, was sound asleep.

By a quarter past seven Charlie was awake again. By

half past he had ripped open all the presents in his stocking and was sitting on the end of his parents' bed surrounded by wrapping paper, his hair sticking up and his eyes shining. Poppy took her time, examining every present before opening the next. A new hoof pick and mane comb, Polos for Cloud and Chester, the latest pony book by her favourite author. Her dad and Caroline sipped tea and watched them indulgently. Once the stockings were opened the McKeevers moved downstairs to the lounge. Charlie shrieked with joy when he saw another pile of presents under the tree. Her dad lit the fire and Poppy and Charlie distributed the presents. Poppy was delighted with a pair of cream jodhpurs, black leather jodhpur boots and a smart blue New Zealand rug for Cloud.

"I thought that he'd be needing a rug soon. It won't be long before his foot is better and you'll be able to turn him out. And you'll be riding him before you know it. You'll need your own jodhpurs and boots then. You can't borrow Scarlett's brother's old ones forever," Caroline said.

Poppy had thought long and hard about what to give Caroline. The answer had come to her as she'd rootled through her jewellery box looking for a silver bangle a couple of weeks earlier. She'd checked with her dad and although he'd looked a bit choked he'd said he thought it was a brilliant idea.

"I hope you like it," she said as she handed the brightly-wrapped present to Caroline. She watched her stepmum's face as she untied the ribbon and prised open the wrapping paper. Inside a layer of white tissue paper was a small silver locket on a simple silver chain. Caroline gasped. "But Poppy, wasn't this your mum's?" she asked, her brows furrowed.

"It was. But it's yours now. I wanted you to have it. Have a look inside."

In one window of the locket was a tiny photo of her dad, taken on holiday the year before. His face was tanned and his hair windswept. He looked every inch the famous BBC news correspondent. In the other window was a picture of Poppy and Charlie, both laughing. Charlie had set the timer on his camera to take the photo, but had taken so many attempts before he'd managed to get the settings right that they'd had a fit of the giggles. Caroline was silent as she studied the photos. Poppy held her breath. What if it had been a terrible mistake and her stepmum hated the thought of wearing Isobel's old locket? But when she looked at Poppy her eyes were bright with tears. "Oh Poppy," she said. "Will you help me put it on?"

Poppy swept her stepmum's blonde hair over one shoulder and fiddled with the two ends of the chain. The clasp closed safely around the final link like two circles on a Venn diagram, indelibly entwined. She hoped the locket would in some small way make up for the years she'd spent giving Caroline the cold shoulder, subconsciously blaming her for her mum's death. There was a wistful look in her dad's eyes. Christmas must be tough for him too, she realised.

"Your mum would have been so proud of you, Poppy," he said, a catch in his voice. "So very proud."

The snow continued to fall, silently and steadily. By the time the McKeevers had demolished a small mountain of bacon sandwiches Riverdale had been blanketed in white. Caroline put the turkey in the oven, wiped her hands on a tea-towel and checked the clock.

"It's half past nine. We've got plenty of time for a walk before I need to put the potatoes on. Though we'd better make sure we have lots of layers on," she said.

A bracing walk on Christmas morning was a McKeever family tradition that went ahead whatever the weather. Poppy could remember Charlie as a baby, bundled up in a white snowsuit, riding in a baby backpack on their dad's shoulders like a Maharaja atop an elephant, as they strolled along the Thames to Richmond and back. When Charlie was older they'd driven up to Richmond Park and watched herds of red and fallow deer grazing below old English oak trees, their branches stark against the pale December sky.

Poppy grabbed a couple of carrots on her way out and called softly to Cloud and Chester from the back door. Their heads appeared over the stable door. "I think I'll turn you out for a couple of hours this morning, Chester." Cloud stamped his foot impatiently and whinnied. "I'm sorry Cloud. I know how desperate you are to go out with him. But it won't be much longer, I promise."

"Look at Freddie! He's gone crazy!" cried Charlie. The McKeevers watched as the dog raced around in circles, flicking sprays of snow into the air with his nose, barking with delight. His joy was contagious and Charlie, his cheeks pink, ran behind him laughing loudly. Poppy lay down and waved her arms and legs in the snow. She sprang up and pointed at the marks she'd made. "Look, a snow angel!"

"So which way are we going to go?" asked her dad.

"Let's walk through Riverdale wood. The stream will look so pretty in all this snow," suggested Caroline, and they set off across the field to the right of the house until they reached the post and rail perimeter fence. Poppy remembered the first time she and Charlie had explored the wood, the day after they'd moved to Riverdale. Then the trees had been heavy with bright green leaves and the air had been warm and still. Now snow flurries swirled around them as they climbed the fence and the bare branches were covered with a layer of white. Charlie led the way, Poppy close behind him. Freddie bounced back and forth, snapping at snowflakes and weaving between them as swiftly as a Prince Philip Cup pony in a bending race.

The McKeevers followed the stream until the trees started to peter out and they emerged onto the open moorland at the base of the tor. A herd of woolly Dartmoor ponies were grazing on the horizon. Just seeing them made Poppy shiver and she wondered if Cloud would have survived the harsh winter had he not been caught in the drift. She fell behind as they skirted the tor and began heading for home. She had the beginnings of a headache and her legs felt leaden. Caroline waited for her to catch up.

"Are you OK Poppy? You look very pale."

"I am a bit tired," Poppy admitted. "The early start must be catching up with me. I don't know how Charlie does it." They watched the six-year-old as he streaked towards them, his red coat as bright as a holly berry against the snow-covered moor. Freddie raced after him, a black and tan shadow at his heels. Charlie slid to a halt a few feet in front of them and clutched his sides dramatically.

"I'm *so* hungry. Can we *please* have Christmas lunch now?"

CHAPTER 25

Before long the McKeevers were pulling crackers and laughing at the terrible cracker jokes.

"What's the best Christmas present in the world?" asked their dad. Everyone shrugged and Charlie, by now completely over-excited, yelled, "I don't know! What *is* the best Christmas present in the world?"

"A broken drum – you just can't beat it," he replied, to a chorus of groans. Caroline and Poppy had decorated the dining room with armfuls of holly and ivy. Candles flickered on the mantelpiece and the table was laden with enough food to feed at least a dozen people. Poppy was sure the roast turkey must smell delicious but she suddenly had no appetite.

"How are you feeling, sweetheart?" asked Caroline, watching her push the food about on her plate.

"Actually, I don't feel too good. Sort of hot and cold at the same time." It was true. One minute she was shivery and the next she was boiling. The thought of eating even a mouthful of turkey made her queasy.

"Sounds like you might be coming down with something. I'll do Cloud and Chester tonight. You stay beside the fire and we'll find a nice film to watch," said Caroline firmly.

By six o'clock Poppy's head was throbbing and she felt overwhelmed with tiredness. Caroline felt her forehead. "You've got a temperature. Come on, let's get you to bed." Once she'd changed into her pyjamas Poppy sank into bed gratefully. Caroline brought her a hot water bottle and a mug of hot lemon and honey.

"I think you've probably come down with the flu. Drink this, it'll make you feel better, and then try to sleep." Caroline bent down to kiss Poppy's forehead. "Sleep tight, sweetheart."

Poppy slept badly. One minute she was throwing off the duvet, her body burning up, the next she was shivering. By morning her throat was raw and her body felt like lead. She doubted she could have stood up if her life depended on it. Caroline brought her a piece of toast and a mug of tea.

"I've mucked out and fed Cloud and Chester. I've turned Chester out for an hour or so. It's been snowing all night so I've put him in the small paddock with a hay net. They are both fine, though missing you," Caroline said. Poppy gave her a wan smile.

The tea and toast sat untouched on her bedside table. She dozed fitfully. Every half an hour or so Caroline, her dad or Charlie would poke their head around the door to see if she needed anything. At lunchtime her dad appeared with a bowl of chicken soup on a tray.

"Caroline says please try to have a little, even if it's only a couple of mouthfuls."

Poppy pulled herself to a sitting position and her dad plumped up the pillows behind her. "I remember doing this for your mum when she had the flu," he said, perching on the end of the bed.

"I don't remember," said Poppy. Her head felt woozy and her muscles ached. She'd never felt so feeble in her life.

"You wouldn't. You were only about six-months-old. Your mum was wiped out for almost a week. I had to look after you both."

"Do you still miss her?" It was the first time she'd ever asked her dad how he felt.

"Of course I do. I always will. But we've been lucky, Poppy. Your mum would have been happy for us, I know she would."

"I do, too."

Later there was a knock at her bedroom door and Caroline called softly, "The doctor's here to see you, Poppy."

She was puzzled. Surely a bout of the flu didn't warrant a home visit by their GP? The door creaked open and there was Charlie, wearing the doctor's dressing up outfit he'd loved when he was four. The arms of the white coat reached his elbows and the plastic stethoscope bounced jauntily on his chest. In his hand he carried a small red case with a white cross.

"Where's the patient?" he asked, walking over to Poppy and feeling her wrist for a pulse. "Yes, she's definitely still alive," he announced with a grin.

"We thought it might make you laugh," said Caroline. "How are you feeling?"

"The same. Is Cloud OK?" she croaked.

"Yes, he's fine. I've just brought Chester in. We're completely snowed in. I haven't even seen a snowplough go past. And there's more snow forecast tonight. Good job we've got plenty of food in. I think it's going to be a few days before we can get the cars out."

"I made an awesome snowman, Poppy," said Charlie. "I wish you were well enough to come and play."

"I'm sorry, Charlie. Maybe I'll be better tomorrow," she said, her head sinking back into the pillows.

"It's OK, you can't help it. Mum says I can feed Cloud and Chester tonight, can't I Mum?"

Caroline smiled. "Yes, you can." She turned to Poppy. "He's desperate to help. I've told him how much they both have."

Poppy nodded. She felt an overwhelming desire to sleep. Noticing her eyelids flutter, Caroline chivvied Charlie out of the room and closed the door gently behind them.

CHAPTER 26

That night Poppy's dreams were vivid. Hope was sitting in a tiny round room at the top of a stone tower, carefully plaiting her long blonde hair as she whispered and giggled with Caitlyn. Caitlyn handed Hope a pretty turquoise box and said to her, 'Inside is the key to Cloud's heart. Use it well'. The image became fuzzy and suddenly Hope was galloping Cloud around the indoor school at Redhall Manor, egged on by Shelley, who was standing in the middle of the school, cracking a lunging whip. Cloud galloped faster and faster, his flared nostrils and the whites of his eyes showing his terror. Poppy, watching from the side, tried to run towards them but it was as if her arms and legs were caught in treacle. She shouted and when Shelley turned around Poppy's blood ran cold. The face staring back at her wasn't Shelley at all. It was George Blackstone. He roared with anger when he saw Poppy and bellowed, 'You thief! You stole my pony!' Poppy tried to run but her legs refused to move. Cloud slowed to a standstill, his flanks heaving. Poppy watched helplessly as his legs buckled beneath him and he fell to the floor with a loud crash.

She woke with a start, her heart thudding. It's a dream, she told herself. But she could still hear crashing and banging. She sat up in bed and tried to identify where the noise was coming from. Apart from the usual creaks and sighs the house was quiet. It seemed to be coming from the stables.

Poppy looked at her clock. Half past four. She slid out of bed and tried standing up. Her legs felt wobbly but at least they worked. She reached for her clothes, dressed quickly and crept downstairs. In the kitchen she grabbed a torch and flung on her hat, gloves and coat. She unlocked the back door and slipped out of the house like a sprite, heading for the stables.

The security light at the back of the house came on as Poppy crunched through the snow to the stables as quickly as she could. As she neared the old stone building she heard a strange grunting noise. Her heart in her mouth, she looked over the stable door. Cloud was standing in the middle of the stable, his head low, breathing rapidly. Chester, standing at the back, hee-hawed loudly when he saw Poppy's frightened face.

"Oh no!' she cried, reaching for the bolts on the door. Cloud sank to the ground and started rolling, his legs thrashing wildly in the air inches from the old donkey, who shrank back into the far corner. Poppy stopped, her head still woozy. I don't know what to do, she thought helplessly. What should I do?

As if sensing her panic Chester hee-hawed again. The sound spurred Poppy into action. She ran into the tack room and grabbed Cloud's headcollar. Within seconds she was edging around the stable trying to avoid his flailing hooves. Once she was behind his head she knelt down and tried to put the headcollar on. But her hands were shaking and every time she got near he jerked his head away.

"Cloud, you must stay still. Just for a minute," she pleaded. For a beat he stopped moving and she grabbed her chance. The headcollar finally on, she stood up and pulled on the leadrope. "Up you get. Come on Cloud, stand up."

Cloud rolled on his back, kicking his stomach, and Poppy tugged again, no thought for her own safety. "You can do this Cloud! Stand up!" He grunted, gathered his legs together and stood up shakily. There was blood on his cheek and his neck was dark with sweat.

Colic. It must be colic, Poppy thought frantically. But what to do? They were completely snowed in – there was no way the vet would get here, even in a Land Rover. She racked her brain, trying to remember what her pony books said. Walking every half an hour, that was it.

"We need to walk, Cloud. To stop you getting a twisted gut." She looked at his foot, encased in its special shoe. "Your foot will have to take its chance. This is more important." He seemed calmed by her voice and she kept talking as she led him slowly out of the stable. Although the back of the house was banked in snow the old stone building had protected the yard from the worst of the drifts and Poppy coaxed the pony up and down the length of it.

"Five minutes' walking every half an hour. I think that's what we need to do," she said, trying to inject some confidence into her voice. Cloud walked slowly, stopping every so often to kick or bite at his stomach. "No, my beautiful boy. You mustn't do that. Keep walking. Please," she begged.

After five freezing minutes she returned him to the stable and investigated the blood on his face. He'd grazed his cheekbone thrashing around in the stable and flinched when Poppy tried to touch it. He was restless and pawed at the ground. He tried to roll again but Poppy held his leadrope firmly and managed to stop him lying down. She checked her watch every couple of minutes and when twenty five minutes had passed she led him back out of the stable for another five minutes of walking. She'd lost all feeling in her feet long ago and her fingers felt icy despite the gloves. Every time Cloud stopped and arched his neck or made the strange grunting noise Poppy felt panic rise up. Horses died of colic. What if Cloud had already twisted his gut? An image of an obscenely pink intestine curling around itself like a giant worm inside her pony's stomach danced in front of her eyes. She shook her head, casting the mirage aside, and concentrated on putting one foot in front of the other. She wondered if she should go for help, wake up Caroline and her dad, call the vet. But the vet would never make it through the snow and there was nothing her dad or Caroline could do. Anyway, she couldn't bear the thought of leaving Cloud, not even for a minute.

The snow kept falling, covering their footprints almost as soon as they had made them. It was as if they were ghosts, already dead, Poppy thought with a shudder. The five minutes were up and she led the pony back into the stable.

How could he have suddenly developed colic? She hadn't changed his food or bedding. He'd seemed perfectly fine on Christmas Day. A bit bored maybe, but that was it. She cursed herself for not checking him on Boxing Day. But she wasn't sure she'd have been able to drag herself out of bed. And then she remembered Charlie in his doctor's outfit, taking her pulse, offering to feed Cloud and Chester. She pictured him in the tack room, lifting the lid on the feed bin nearest the door, not realising that Poppy had re-arranged everything when she'd had her big clear out. Not noticing that the pony nuts were in fact unsoaked cubes of sugar beet…

Poppy thought she was hallucinating again when Cloud curled his lip up at her as if he was laughing, as if he thought it was all a massive joke. But she remembered it was another symptom of colic, and stroked his neck gently, murmuring to him softly. Chester watched them from the corner of the stable, his brown eyes sadder than she'd ever seen them. He knew, she thought wildly. He knew that Cloud was going to die. She checked her watch. Half past five. Another fifteen minutes and she'd take him out again. Cloud's legs started buckling as he prepared to sink down and roll.

"Cloud, no!" she shouted in alarm. "Stand up, you must stand!" She grabbed the cheek straps of his headcollar and, with a superhuman effort, hauled him to a standing position. He gave an almighty shake, the leadrope rattling in her hands. Poppy felt waves of desolation and exhaustion wash over her.

"Don't die, Cloud. Please don't die," she sobbed. But the pony looked defeated, his head low and his eyes dull.

She wrapped her arms around his neck and howled.

CHAPTER 27

"Poppy! What on earth -?"

Caroline's anxious voice roused Poppy from her torpor. She looked up and saw her stepmother's white face over the stable door.

"It's Cloud," she said flatly. "He's got colic. He's dying."

"*What?*"

"I heard him crashing about in his stable last night. He was in agony. I walked him up and down like you're supposed to but it was no good. I couldn't save him. Just like I couldn't save him from the drift." Poppy's voice was hoarse, her face wet with tears.

"But Poppy -" Caroline began.

"It's my fault. If I hadn't moved the feed bins around Charlie wouldn't have got the sugar beet mixed up with the pony nuts and everything would have been alright. It's all my fault," she repeated, her voice a monotone.

"I'll call the vet. Maybe there's a chance she can get here."

"There's no point. He's twisted his gut, you see," Poppy continued, looking at her stepmother with puffy eyes. "He can't have long left." She swallowed a sob.

Caroline took in the scene before her. Poppy, purple shadows under her eyes and her face drawn, propped against Cloud. The grey pony stood as still as a statue, his eyes on Caroline. At the back of the stable Chester's head was drooping as he dozed. The straw bedding looked as if it had been whipped up and flung around by a band of whirling dervishes. A pile of fresh droppings on the stable floor steamed in the cold.

"Are you sure?" Caroline pressed.

"Of course I'm sure. I'm staying with him until the end. I promised him I'd never leave him."

Caroline suddenly found it difficult to speak. In that moment she knew she loved her shy, complicated stepdaughter as if she were her own. Poppy could be insecure and stubborn, but her courage and loyalty took Caroline's breath away. She let herself into the stable and touched Poppy lightly on the shoulder. The girl looked up, her face anguished. She took two shaky steps towards Caroline and buried herself in her stepmother's arms, her body racked with sobs.

"Oh sweetheart, don't upset yourself. It breaks my

heart to see you like this," she whispered.

"I'm going to lose him. I can't bear it."

But something was niggling Caroline. As her gaze swept over the stable for a second time her face cleared.

"Poppy, Cloud's been to the toilet. Look!"

Poppy shrugged, broke away from Caroline's embrace and wiped her tear-streaked cheeks. "So?"

"Don't you see? The blockage in his gut must have shifted. It means the worst of the colic has passed. Quickly, see if he wants a drink."

Poppy still looked dazed so Caroline picked up the closest water bucket and held it under Cloud's nose. He sniffed it cautiously then drank thirstily. He finished half the bucket and snorted loudly, spraying Caroline with droplets of water. She laughed. "See? You did exactly the right thing, Poppy. You saved him!"

They stood together and watched Cloud. After ten minutes or so he edged over to the hayrack and pulled out a couple of wisps of hay. When he lifted his tail and deposited another mound of steaming manure by their welly-clad feet they clutched each other in joy.

"I'll call the vet anyway, just to be on the safe side. Even if she can't make it out here she can give us some advice on the phone. But I think he's going to be fine, Poppy. Thanks to you."

Poppy was just about to reply when the ground shifted beneath her feet and her head felt so light she thought it might float away. The last thing she noticed before she lost consciousness were black spots dancing in front of her eyes and a ringing in her ears.

When she woke up she was back in bed, the worried faces of her dad, Caroline and Charlie looming over her.

"You fainted. Not surprising really. You're recovering from the flu, you've been up half the night and you haven't eaten for forty eight hours," said Caroline. She offered Poppy a mug of tea. "It's got plenty of sugar in it. Please try to have some."

Poppy sat up in a panic, almost sending the mug flying.

"Cloud? Is he OK?"

"Yes, he's fine. I've phoned the vet and explained everything. She's happy. We've just got to keep an eye on him over the next day or so."

Relieved, Poppy took the tea and sipped. Caroline and her dad left the room but Charlie stayed. He hovered by the door, red-eyed. When he eventually spoke his voice was small.

"I'm sorry I gave Cloud the wrong nuts, Poppy. I didn't mean to give him tummy ache."

"It wasn't your fault. You were only trying to help. I should have told you I'd moved the bins about. You weren't to know. And he's alright, so there's nothing to be sorry about."

Charlie didn't look convinced.

"Honestly Charlie, it's OK. Want to come for a cuddle?"

He stuck his thumb in his mouth and nodded. Poppy patted the bed and he sidled over.

"What would cheer you up?" she said, as she wriggled up the bed and put her arm around his shoulders.

Charlie thought for a moment. "A snowball fight?" he said hopefully. "I think that would probably do it."

Poppy laughed. He really was incorrigible.

"It's a deal. But first I must have breakfast. I'm so hungry I could eat -"

"A horse?" her brother suggested.

"No!" Poppy pretended to be outraged and was glad to see Charlie giggle.

"A full English breakfast, is what I was going to say. Sausages, bacon, tomatoes, mushrooms, a fried egg," she listed, ticking each off on her fingers. "Oh, and toast. Loads and loads of toast."

Only once Poppy had seen for herself that Cloud was settled and eating normally again did she agree to sit down and have breakfast, by which time her stomach was growling ominously.

"I hope I haven't made his fracture worse," she said, as she demolished an enormous plateful of food.

"You did exactly the right thing," replied Caroline firmly. "OK, so even if he has damaged his foot the worst case scenario is more box rest. But the vet didn't seem to think walking up and down in the snow every half an hour would have made a huge difference. In fact she said he was more likely to have made it worse thrashing and banging about in the stable. So stop worrying. And that's an order," she added, waving a spatula at Poppy.

Poppy knew her stepmother was probably right and for once she let herself feel optimistic. Her phone bleeped.

"It's Scarlett. She wants to know if we'd like to go tobogganing at Ashworthy. Can we go?" Poppy asked.

"Only if I can come, too. I used to love tobogganing when I was your age. There weren't many chances to do it in London. I might even try to drag your dad along. He could do with the exercise," her stepmother answered.

The family spent the next couple of hours climbing up and whizzing down Ashworthy's top sheep field on plastic fertiliser sacks filled with snow, shrieking with glee as they sped feet first down the hill and laughing wildly as they collided in a heap at the bottom.

Pat invited them to stay for lunch and as they squeezed around the pine table in the kitchen they regaled her and Bill with stories of hotly-contested races and spectacular tumbles. Pat had made two vast dishes of cauliflower cheese which they mopped up with chunky slices of granary bread. Despite her massive breakfast Poppy was ravenous and was soon having second helpings.

Conversation drifted from sledging to her dad's trip to Syria. The room was silent as he described his life as a war correspondent.

"It must be difficult not to get too emotionally involved," observed Bill from the head of the table.

"It is, sometimes," her dad admitted. "I'm supposed to be objective, to be an observer, but it is hard, especially when children are involved."

"Speaking of which, how's young Hope Taylor?" asked Pat.

"Oh, she's still in remission, isn't she Poppy?" said Caroline. Poppy shot a glance at Scarlett, who was listening intently.

"I save all my two pound coins and give them to a different charity every year. Last year we gave more than £300 to the RSPCA. I thought I'd like to donate them to the Hope for Hope Appeal this year," said Pat.

Across the table Scarlett made a strange gurgling noise as she choked on a piece of cauliflower. Her dad patted her on the back. "That's a nice idea, love," he told his wife.

Poppy looked at the kind, open faces of Pat and Bill. Farming was a tough business and she knew they sometimes struggled to make ends meet. She thought about the piles of dog biscuits she and Scarlett had spent hours baking and Tory's £500 cheque, all the quiz nights and raffles. It was no good. This had to stop.

CHAPTER 28

Over the next 24 hours the snow disappeared almost as quickly as it had arrived. Mild westerly winds coaxed the temperatures above freezing and soon the countryside had shed its white winter coat and was green once more. Poppy checked Cloud obsessively but he seemed to have made a full recovery and if anything was more impatient than ever to escape the confines of his stable. Letting Chester out each morning had become a two person job – one to lead out the old donkey and the other to police the stable door to stop Cloud barging his way out behind him. When Poppy laid a palm on Cloud's dappled grey flank she fancied she could actually feel the pent-up energy pulsing through his veins in time to her own heartbeat. Poppy, back to full strength, was also restless, although she couldn't say why. The only time she felt settled was in Cloud's company. He, too, was less edgy when they were together so she spent hours in his stable, grooming him, tacking him up and dreaming of the day she could jump on his back and they could ride off into the sunset together, as if they were the stars in their own cheesy film.

The start of term was looming when Shelley called Caroline asking if she could look after Hope while she went to London for the day.

"Off to see the cancer specialist again is she?" asked Poppy cynically. "Funny, isn't it, how she always comes back from seeing Hope's *oncologist*," Poppy emphasised the word heavily, "with a new outfit and hairdo."

"Poppy!" said Caroline, shocked. "The appeal's nearly reached its £10,000 target, apparently, so she's going up to finalise details of their trip to America."

"I bet she is," muttered Poppy under her breath, remembering the holiday brochure Shelley had kicked under the sofa at Flint Cottage.

Either Caroline hadn't heard or she had chosen to ignore Poppy's remark. "I can't believe how quickly they've raised the money. People have been so generous. But then it is such a great cause. Think how wonderful it would be for Hope and Shelley if the treatment works this time."

"What time is she dropping Hope off?" Poppy asked, knowing she must seize this chance to tackle her friend while Shelley was well out of the way.

Caroline looked at her watch. "In about half an hour. I've got to go to the supermarket later so you can have an hour in Tavistock together if you like. You don't mind, do you?"

"No, it'll be good to catch up. I haven't had a proper chat with Hope for ages," she said.

Poppy was in the stable grooming Cloud when she heard Shelley's engine revving and a car door slamming. She let herself out and met Hope as she appeared around the corner of the house.

"Poppy! Your mum told me about the colic. It must have been terrifying. How is he?"

"Better now, thanks."

The concern in Hope's pale blue eyes appeared genuine and Poppy wondered yet again if she'd got it all wrong. It was all so far-fetched.

"Can I give you a hand?" Hope asked, interrupting her thoughts.

"Uh, yes, sure. You brush his tail while I do his mane. He's still a bit head shy with people he doesn't know so well." Poppy picked up the comb and began running it through Cloud's silver mane, teasing out the knots and tangles as gently as she could. As she combed she wished life was as easy to untangle.

They worked in silence for a few minutes before Poppy cleared her throat and took the plunge. "So, how are you feeling?"

"I'm OK. Same as usual," Hope answered, uncertainly.

"Yes, you're looking well. The picture of health, some might say."

"Poppy, you're being a bit weird. Is something wrong?"

"You tell me, Hope. I don't want to sound unsympathetic but you don't seem very ill to me."

Hope didn't reply but her face was flustered.

"I was thinking this morning how generous everyone has been towards you and your appeal," Poppy continued, her jaw tight. "Tory gave her washing machine money, Dad and Caroline gave a couple of hundred pounds, Pat and Bill are donating their coin collection and Scarlett and I spent hours baking dog biscuits to raise money. That's just the people I know about. Hundreds of others have been raising money. Sponsored walks, boot fairs, quiz nights, you name it, they've organised it. Remind me, what's it all been for?"

"Mum's appeal," Hope whispered so quietly that Poppy had to strain to hear.

"Yes, the appeal. That's right. But what's the appeal actually paying for? Specialist cancer treatment in California, or a holiday in Florida? And let's not forget the flash telly and the spanking new outfits your mum seems to be wearing every time I see her. What's really going on, Hope?"

"You already know this, Poppy. I have an aggressive form of leukaemia. It's a cancer of the blood. Doctors here say it's terminal but there's a new treatment in America that's going to cure me," Hope intoned. It was as if she'd learnt the script by rote.

"So you say. But I'm afraid I don't believe you."

Poppy slipped a hand in her pocket and fingered the folded sheet of A4 paper she'd printed out at Lizzie's house in Bromley.

"This is your last chance to come clean, Hope. I want you to tell me the truth."

"I don't know what you mean," Hope blustered.

Poppy pulled out the printout, unfolded it with exaggerated care and held it out to Hope. "Take it," she ordered, her voice grim. "It's from the Croydon News four years ago. I want you to read it. Although I have a feeling you already know what it says."

She watched Hope's face for a reaction. If she'd needed any convincing that her theory was right the evidence was there in front of her. Guilt was written all over Hope's thin face.

CHAPTER 29

Hope shrank back against the wall of the stable, her eyes glistening with tears. She glanced at the printout and shook her head.

"Please, no," she whispered.

"Have it your way," said Poppy. "I'll tell you what it says, shall I?"

Poppy had read the newspaper report so many times she could have probably recited it from memory.

"A Croydon woman who shaved a girl's head in an elaborate cancer scam has been told she was lucky to escape jail.

"Michelle Turner pretended the six-year-old had leukaemia and set up a £5,000 appeal to raise money to send her to America for life-saving treatment.

"But the 32-year-old's story was nothing more than a web of lies, prosecutor Daniel Watkins told Croydon Magistrates'

Court on Thursday.

"Turner admitted fraud and was given a six month suspended prison sentence. Magistrates also ordered her to pay more than £5,000 in compensation. The money will be returned to everyone who donated to her bogus appeal.

"The deception began almost a year ago when Turner took the girl, who cannot be named for legal reasons, out of school for a month. Turner claimed the six-year-old was in hospital having aggressive chemotherapy and when she returned to school she had lost all her hair.

"But the court heard that Turner had shaved the girl's head to give her story credibility and had pocketed all the cash donated by concerned well-wishers.

"'It was a particularly cynical scam that took advantage of people's generosity,' Mr Watkins told the court."

Poppy paused for breath. Hope had slid down the wall and was sitting on the straw in a ball, her hands covering her ears. Poppy felt anger bubbling inside her.

"Michelle Turner and Shelley Taylor are the same person, aren't they? And you were that girl, weren't you Hope? How could you do it to us all? Deep down I've known something was wrong for weeks. It just took me a while to realise what it was. I still can't believe anyone could be so deceitful."

A tear rolled down Hope's cheek.

"It was something Charlie said that made me start to realise what was going on. He said you didn't look very ill to him. But you'd lost your hair because of the chemo so this cancer business must be true. So why have you still got eyebrows?"

Hope reached up involuntarily and felt one eyebrow with her index finger. Her face filled with horror.

"Then I remembered the shaving cream and razors in your bathroom cabinet. I don't think you lost your hair through chemotherapy at all, did you Hope? I've been checking, you see. According to the cancer websites you'd have lost your eyebrows, too. And someone's hair almost always grows back when they've finished their chemo, and yours has had plenty of time to grow back. I started thinking your mum might have been shaving your head to make it look as though you were having chemotherapy, but she's so dense she forgot to shave your eyebrows. I was beginning to wonder if you even had cancer at all."

Hope lifted her head and tried to speak, but Poppy was on a roll. She was pacing up and down like a detective in a daytime television crime drama. "Then Scarlett and I saw your mum with George Blackstone at the Waterby Dog Show. You remember, when we were selling all those biscuits we made to raise money for your fund?"

Hope flinched.

"Shelley and George were as thick as thieves. Which is pretty apt in the circumstances, I think you'll agree. They definitely looked far too cosy to be landlord and tenant. So that also got me thinking.

And then Tory told me that George Blackstone had a niece who'd moved away from Waterby when she was a child and never came back. But what if she had, thirty years later, and she turned out to be as scheming as her uncle?"

"Poppy-" Hope began, her voice a strangulated whisper. But Poppy ignored her.

"I remembered the envelope addressed to Mrs M. Turner that turned up at your house. I'd assumed it must have been for the old lady who used to live there, but I checked. She was Mrs Deakins. I tried Googling Mrs M. Turner but there were thousands of hits. Then I remembered Shelley can be short for Michelle. So I tapped in Michelle Turner and Croydon and bingo. The top hit was the Croydon News report. And then I knew I was one hundred per cent right."

The walls of the stable felt as though they were closing in and Poppy reached for Cloud's solid bulk seeking reassurance, but he turned away from her and headed for his hayrack. She had a horrible feeling she'd gone too far. Hope was sobbing uncontrollably now and Poppy felt something inside her shift. The anger dissipated as quickly as it had come and there was a catch in her voice when she finally spoke again. "I thought you were my friend."

Hope wiped her tear-stained cheeks. "You don't understand," she stammered. "Mum made me do it. I had no choice."

"How do I know you're telling the truth now when

everything else you've told me has been a pack of lies?" Poppy demanded.

"I wanted to tell you, Poppy, I really did. But Mum said if we got caught she'd be sent to prison and I'd end up in care."

"What about your dad?"

"He left when she was arrested last time. He said he couldn't put up with her any more. I begged him to take me with him but he couldn't. He was living in a bedsit and there wasn't enough room for me. Then he emigrated to Canada. He promised me that once he was settled I could go and live with him but Mum told me he'd changed his mind once he met Kirstin and didn't want me. I've been so happy here, making friends with you and Scarlett, learning to ride and everything. The last thing I wanted to do was pretend I had cancer again."

Poppy remembered the conversation she'd overheard in the shop. Perhaps Hope hadn't wanted to go along with Shelley's plans. But she still wasn't satisfied.

"You could have told me. I would have helped, you know."

"I didn't want to do it, Poppy. You have to believe me. We got chucked out of our flat in Croydon because Mum was behind on the rent. She was always talking about her Uncle George and how he was rolling in money. I heard her on the phone to him one night and the next morning she told me we were moving into one of his farm cottages. I was so happy.

I've always wanted to live in the country. I thought it might be a fresh start for me and Mum. Then when we arrived she said we needed some cash while she tried to find a job and I'd have to pretend I had cancer again. I pleaded with her not to but she refused to listen."

Poppy had to admit it made sense. "OK, maybe I do believe you. But we have to do something. Your mum can't go on conning people out of money. We need to report her to the police."

"We can't! She'll go to prison and I'll end up in care! She promised she would stop as soon as she reached ten thousand pounds. We were going to go to America and when we came back she was going to let my hair grow back and tell everyone the treatment had worked."

Hope cradled her head in her hands and rocked on her heels. Poppy knelt down in the straw beside her and put an arm around her shoulder. "It's OK, Hope. We'll do it together. Your mum won't be able to force you to do anything ever again."

"No Poppy, I won't." She lifted her head and sniffed loudly. "I *can't.*"

CHAPTER 30

Hope looked Poppy straight in the eye. "I'm frightened of her, Poppy. I'm frightened of what she might do if she finds out I've told someone again. That's why I'm not allowed to go to school. I told my teacher last time, you see. I let it slip that my mum shaved my head. School told the police and Mum was arrested. She went absolutely ballistic."

Poppy remembered the conversation they'd almost had on the Riverdale tor.

"Has she ever hurt you, Hope?"

"She sometimes yanks my arm when she loses her temper but it's only when I've done something wrong, dropped something or made a mess, you know?"

Poppy shook her head in disbelief. She couldn't even begin to imagine the tightrope Hope must walk every day.

"She's never actually hit me. And it's my fault she gets cross."

"Normal people don't behave like that, Hope. No mum should take out their anger on their child, or force them to do something they don't want to do. I'm sorry but people like your mum never change. How can you be sure that one day she won't lose her temper and lash out at you?"

Hope had no answer.

"You can't let her get away with it. We need to tell the police." Poppy thought for a moment. How could she convince Hope to do the right thing?

"What would your dad tell you to do if he was here?"

Hope sniffed. "Go to the police," she whispered.

"Then that's what we must do. We'll do it together. It'll all be OK, you'll see."

"Do you promise?"

Poppy gave her a squeeze. "Yes. I promise."

They heard the back door slam and Charlie's head appeared over the stable door seconds later.

"What do you want?" Poppy sighed.

"Mum sent me to tell you…hold on, why are Hope's eyes so red?"

"Hayfever," supplied Poppy, hoping the six-year-old wouldn't remember it was mid-winter.

"Oh. It looks like she's been crying, that's all. Anyway, Mum says she's going into town in half an hour so you need to come and get ready."

Once he'd gone Poppy handed Hope a tissue and she blew her nose noisily.

"We'll go to the police station while Caroline's in the supermarket. We'll ask to see whoever's in charge and explain everything. They'll know what to do," said Poppy, more confidently than she felt.

Hope sat silently chewing her nails during the drive to Tavistock. Poppy tried valiantly to keep the conversation going. It was at times like these that you really needed Scarlett's easy chatter, she thought. Caroline glanced at Hope in the rear-view mirror.

"Everything OK, sweetheart?" she asked. Hope, who had been staring at the passing countryside, gave a start.

"Oh, yes. I'm fine thank you," she answered quietly. Caroline seemed satisfied. Poppy fidgeted in her seat and wondered if they should have told Caroline first. But what if her stepmum decided to tackle Shelley herself? Poppy was convinced that Shelley would vanish, taking Hope with her, at the merest hint of trouble. And she had given Hope her word that everything would be alright.

"I'll be at least an hour. Shall I meet you back at the car at about four?" asked Caroline, as they turned into the supermarket car park.

"Yes. We're going to go and have a look around the Pannier Market, aren't we Hope?" said Poppy. She gave Hope a nudge.

"What? Oh yes, the Pannier Market," she said.

"And don't forget –" Caroline began.

"Yes, I know Mum. Be careful crossing the roads, stick together and text if we're running late," Poppy finished.

Caroline smiled and disappeared in search of a trolley leaving the two girls in the car park, their faces grave.

"I know it probably doesn't feel like it but the sooner we get this over with the better. Come on, let's go," said Poppy and she started marching towards the police station, Hope following reluctantly behind.

They hadn't expected to queue but when they pushed open the heavy door an elderly man in a tweed jacket was leaning against the counter in the small reception area. He was talking loudly to a female police officer. Poppy could see a hearing aid in his right ear.

"So when did you last see your wallet, Mr Bristow?" asked the PC, enunciating carefully.

The old man spluttered, "If I knew that I wouldn't be here, would I? It's lost, that's the point. Has anyone handed it in?"

The PC glanced up at the newcomers and flashed them a smile. She looked kind and capable. Suddenly Poppy knew it was going to be OK. She and Hope stood patiently while the PC took down the pensioner's details and Poppy opened the door for him as he left. He gave her a curt nod and was gone.

"Mr Bristow loses his wallet at least once a month but it always turns up, usually in the most unexpected places. Last time he found it in his potting shed. The time before that it was in his freezer," said the PC. She looked at Poppy closely. "I know you, don't I? You're the girl from Waterby who got lost on the moor. Poppy something. McKendrick, wasn't it?"

"McKeever," said Poppy. "That's right. I was looking for my brother Charlie."

The PC looked pleased with herself. "I never forget a face. I was with your mum at the hospital while the search and rescue teams were looking for you. She was so relieved when they found you both. I'm PC Claire Bodiam. What can I do for you two?"

Poppy looked at Hope's pale face and took a deep breath. "Is there somewhere we can talk in private? We want to report a crime."

PC Bodiam led them into an interview room behind the front counter.

"I want you to take your time and tell me what's happened," she said, sitting down opposite them, her pocket notebook open. She listened silently as Poppy began talking. When Poppy produced the newspaper printout from her pocket she held up her hand.

"I think my guvnor needs to hear this. He's in a meeting upstairs. I'll see if I can interrupt it." As she left the room Poppy noticed Hope was on the verge of tears.

"I don't think I can do this. Mum'll never forgive me, I know she won't."

"It'll be alright," soothed Poppy. "I trust PC

Bodiam. She'll know what to do for the best."

When the PC returned she was with an older police officer who introduced himself as Inspector Bill Pearson. His ruddy face was cheerful and his shirt strained over his large stomach. He looked more like a farmer than a police inspector, thought Poppy.

"Right, what about a cup of tea before we start," he said. "There's a new packet of biscuits in the rest room. Bring them down won't you, Claire?" He patted his belly. "I really shouldn't but I can't resist a couple of digestives with my tea. My wife keeps trying to put me on a diet but I think it's a bit late for all that, don't you? Now what's all this about the Hope for Hope Appeal?"

Half an hour later Poppy had explained everything. Inspector Pearson had listened intently and PC Bodiam had taken copious notes.

"So when is your mum due home?" the inspector asked Hope.

"About six o'clock I think. Caroline – that's Poppy's stepmum – was going to drop me back after tea at about half past."

"Now Hope, I want to assure you that you aren't in any trouble. You've done absolutely the right thing coming here to tell us what's happened and I don't want you to be in any doubt about that," said Inspector Pearson, helping himself to his third digestive.

"What will happen to my mum?"

"You leave that to us. Do you have any other

family apart from your mum who could look after you for a short while?"

"There's Great Uncle George, but please don't make me stay there. My dad lives in Canada. I've got his mobile number if you want it."

PC Bodiam nodded. "Yes, let me have the number and I'll contact him now."

"Hope can stay with us while everything's sorted out," said Poppy. She looked at the clock over the door. It was five to four. "We're supposed to be meeting my stepmum at the supermarket at four. I'd better text her to let her know where we are."

Poppy tapped out a quick message. *We're at the police station. Can you meet us there? NOTHING TO WORRY ABOUT! Xxx*

Caroline arrived less than five minutes later, bursting through the front door, her face anxious. Her expression turned from disbelief to indignation as Inspector Pearson filled her in on Shelley's exploits.

"To think I convinced Tory to give £500 to the appeal! I can't believe I was so naïve," she said.

"Don't worry, you're not the only one. Hundreds of others have been taken in. Unfortunately individuals like Ms Taylor rely on people's generosity for their scams to work. She isn't the first person to take good, honest people for a ride, and I'm afraid she won't be the last," the inspector told her.

Hope hugged herself tightly, her head bowed, as she listened to the exchange. Caroline lifted her chin gently. "You poor love. No-one's going to blame you. And you can stay with us for as long as you need to." She was rewarded with a weak smile.

Inspector Pearson stood up, signalling that the interview was over. "There are things I need to be seeing to. PC Bodiam will see you out. And keep Mrs McKeever informed of events, won't you, Claire?"

"Yes, boss."

CHAPTER 31

After that things happened quickly. Inspector Pearson briefed a small team of detectives who spoke to their counterparts in Croydon. They confirmed that Shelley Taylor and Michelle Turner were indeed one and the same. The Hope for Hope Appeal bank account was frozen and an arrest warrant issued. When Shelley arrived at Flint Cottage just before six o'clock, clutching several designer carrier bags, she was greeted by two detectives, who drove her to Plymouth for questioning. PC Bodiam called Riverdale just after eight to say Shelley was being held in custody overnight and was due to appear before magistrates in the morning charged with fraud offences.

"She's made a full and frank admission," PC Bodiam told Caroline. "Maybe she's seen the error of her ways, maybe she's hoping the magistrates will be lenient if she pleads guilty at the first opportunity, who knows? She's a slippery customer. But she's almost certainly going to get a prison term because of her previous conviction. I'd say she was looking at three years inside, minimum. And can you let Hope know that I've spoken to her dad? He's catching the first available flight out of Toronto and is hoping to be in the country by tomorrow evening."

"That's fantastic news, I'll let her know. Will Hope have to give evidence in court?" asked Caroline.

"I would imagine the court would be happy with a written statement from her, especially as Shelley is pleading guilty. And Hope's anonymity will be protected because she's a minor."

Caroline ended the call and updated Poppy and Hope. Hope had discarded her wig and she looked younger than ever. Her eyes shone when she heard that her dad was on his way.

"See?" Poppy said. "I told you everything would be OK."

While Caroline made up the camp bed in Poppy's room and found Hope some of her old pyjamas, Poppy slipped out of the back door to see Cloud. She had the sense that he'd understood exactly what was going on in the stable that afternoon and hadn't approved of the way Poppy had tackled Hope. He was lying down in the straw, his legs tucked under him, his eyelids heavy. Chester was rootling around by their buckets hunting for any stray pony nuts. Poppy sat down and draped her arm around Cloud's neck.

"I know you think I was too hard on Hope, Cloud, but I was so angry she'd lied to me. You were right though, I should have realised it was all Shelley's idea and Hope wasn't to blame. But I've apologised to her and we're friends again." She stroked Cloud's nose absentmindedly and he blew gently into her hand, his warm breath tickling her fingers. She felt forgiven.

Hope's dad arrived at Riverdale the following evening, dishevelled after a night flight from Toronto. Hope tore through the house like a mini-hurricane when she heard his taxi and hurled herself into his arms.

He introduced himself to the McKeevers. "Matt Taylor. Pleased to meet you. Sorry it's not under better circumstances. Hope, I wish you'd told me what was happening."

"I couldn't, Dad. Mum said she'd be put in prison and I'd end up in a children's home if anyone found out. She said you didn't want me any more, not now you had Kirstin and your new life in Canada." Hope buried her face in his jumper.

"Your mum said a lot of things that weren't true, Hope. But things are going to change. Kirstin and I want you to come and live with us."

"In Canada?"

"Yes. No-one will know about your mum and what she's done there. It'll be a new start. Would you like that?"

"More than anything. Though I'll miss everyone

here. Especially Buster. He's the pony I've been having riding lessons on," she explained.

"There are riding schools in Canada, you know," laughed her dad. I'm sure we can sort something out."

Once again Shelley Taylor was front page news in the Tavistock Herald. But this time it was for all the wrong reasons. Her court case was heard quickly and, despite her guilty plea, magistrates jailed her for three-and-a-half years. Fortunately Hope wasn't around to see the story. The day before the paper came out she flew to Canada with her dad. Away from Shelley's clutches she had morphed into the bright, fun-loving girl Poppy had seen glimpses of during their time together.

"I'm going to miss you all so much," she told the McKeevers. "Especially you, Poppy. You will keep in touch, won't you? I want to know how Cloud and Chester are doing. And Buster and Rosie. Can you thank Bella for me? I feel bad that she gave me those lessons because she thought I had cancer."

"It wasn't your fault, Hope. Bella will understand. And everyone who gave to the appeal will get their money back. So stop apologising!" Poppy ordered with a grin.

It felt strange saying goodbye to Hope for the last time. "We've only known her for a few months but it seems much longer than that," Poppy said to Caroline as they watched the Taylors' taxi disappear down the drive.

"I know what you mean. She feels like part of the family. I wonder how Shelley's coping in prison. It's terrible that she's going to miss out on so many years of Hope's childhood."

Poppy raised her eyebrows. Her dad spoke firmly. "Spare your sympathy for someone who deserves it, Caroline. Shelley was quite happy to con little old ladies out of their hard-earned savings. She had it coming to her."

Perfectly put, thought Poppy, watching her dad link arms with Caroline and walk back into the house. Although she wasn't sure Tory would have appreciated being called a little old lady.

The last few days of the Christmas holidays flew by and before she knew it Poppy was sitting on the school bus next to Scarlett on the first day of term. After being given the first few months to find their feet, Poppy, Scarlett and the rest of the Year Sevens were suddenly disappearing under a mountain of homework. Her dad had managed to secure a temporary secondment to the BBC's foreign desk in London and left Riverdale at four every Monday morning, returning home late every Friday night. Poppy's riding lessons at Redhall Manor were still a highlight of her week. Under Bella's expert tutelage she was learning how to slow Rosie to a collected trot and canter and then lengthen her strides into extended paces. With Hope gone, Poppy had Bella's full attention and the riding school owner didn't miss a trick. If Poppy wasn't being chided for rounding her shoulders Bella was castigating her for not maintaining contact with Rosie's mouth. Sometimes Poppy wondered if she was making any progress at all. She treasured any nuggets of praise, however small, and the day Bella told her she was a tidy little rider she virtually floated home.

The first snowdrops were flowering in time for Poppy's twelfth birthday. It fell on a Sunday and Caroline woke early to pick Poppy a small bunch of the waxy white flowers from where they grew in drifts in the border next to her vegetable garden. Delicate in appearance yet tough enough to push their way through frozen soil, the snowdrops reminded Caroline of her stepdaughter. She arranged them in a small vase on a tray with some croissants and honey. Treating Poppy to breakfast in bed was not something she would have felt able to do a year ago. Poppy would have rejected the attempt to reach out to her. It still gladdened her heart that they had moved on so far since then.

As she approached Poppy's bedroom, Charlie bounded out, his hair tousled.

"She's still asleep," he told his mum in a stage whisper.

"I was," came Poppy's voice from behind her door, "Until you sneaked in and trod on Magpie's tail and he squealed and woke me up."

Charlie grinned at Caroline. "Oops," he said. "Is

Dad awake?"

Soon they were all sitting on the end of Poppy's bed watching the birthday girl eat her croissants. When she'd finished Charlie ran out again only to reappear with a pile of presents in his arms, which he deposited on his sister's lap.

"Open mine first," he demanded, waving a rectangular parcel under her nose.

"OK, OK!" she laughed. Charlie had used so much sticky tape it took Poppy a good five minutes to peel open the wrapping paper. She pulled off the last strip to reveal two wooden name plates.

"I remembered we saw some in Baxters' but I didn't have enough pocket money to buy them so I made my own. There's one for Cloud and one for Chester. I painted their names and they've both got their pictures on. Mum did the outlines and I coloured them in," Charlie said proudly.

With Charlie's spidery handwriting and inexpertly coloured heads that were only vaguely equine-shaped, they were a far cry from the professionally painted and varnished name plates in Baxters' Animal Feeds. But Poppy didn't mind.

"They're brilliant! Thank you Charlie. I'll hang them on the stable door later."

Her dad handed her a large, flat present. "I hope you like it. We didn't really know what to get you, what with your birthday so close to Christmas."

Poppy tore off the paper. Inside a layer of bubble wrap was a framed watercolour of Cloud and Chester in the shadow of the Riverdale tor. The pony and donkey stood looking straight at her, perfectly captured in time. She traced her finger across Cloud's neck and smiled. It was a beautiful painting.

"Caroline heard about a local artist who specialises in horses and commissioned him to paint it," said her dad.

"It's amazing. How did he get such a good likeness?" Poppy wondered.

"I took dozens of photos and emailed them to him," said Caroline. "Then one day while you were at school he drove over and did some sketches. Do you like it?"

"I *love* it. Thank you so much," she said, flinging her arms around her stepmum and blowing her dad a kiss.

"So what does twelve feel like?" he asked her.

"Absolutely ancient," groaned Poppy.

It was a wonderful start to a perfect day. When Poppy went down to feed and muck out Cloud and Chester she found another present hidden in their hayrack. The label read, *To Poppy, our favourite human in the whole world. With all our love, Cloud and Chester xx.* Inside were a body protector and a pair of leather riding gloves.

While she was sweeping the yard Scarlett turned up riding Blaze and leading Flynn.

"Happy birthday, Poppy. It's time to down tools and come for a ride. Here's your mount for the day," she said, handing Flynn's reins to Poppy. "I think you'll agree he's been beautifully groomed for the occasion."

Once Poppy had raced inside to change the two girls headed onto the moor for their favourite hack, a two hour ride that followed the valley towards the Blackstone farm before skirting a copse and returning along quiet country lanes. Scarlett craned her neck as they passed Flint Cottage but there was nothing to see. The curtains were drawn and the house had a desolate, forsaken look about it. But it had never been a happy place, thought Poppy.

"I wonder how Hope's getting on," said Scarlett, reading her mind.

"I had a birthday email from her this morning. She's due to start school in the next couple of days and said she's really looking forward to it. Her dad's already found a riding school near them and she's going to have lessons once a week. Oh, and she really likes Kirstin, that's her dad's girlfriend."

"So it all worked out for the best in the end."

"Shelley might not agree. She's in prison in Gloucestershire, according to a story in the Herald this week."

"She deserved everything she got," said Scarlett firmly, kicking Blaze into a trot.

That evening, just before seven o'clock, Scarlett sent Poppy a text. *Dad says would you and Charlie like to see a lamb being born? He's got a ewe due to deliver in the next hour xxx.*

Caroline walked with them across the field to Ashworthy. All the ewes were in a large barn at the far side of the farmyard. Scarlett was already there watching her dad checking over a black-faced ewe that was pawing the ground and panting. Charlie was clutching his digital camera in one hand and his binoculars in the other.

"This is so exciting. It's like a real life nature documentary," he whispered.

"Aye, all we need now is David Attenborough and a camera crew to appear," chuckled Bill.

"Don't worry, Bill. My camera does short films as well. How long will we have to wait before the lamb is born? I'll need to get into position."

"I don't think she'll be long now, lad," Bill told the six-year-old. He was right. The ewe lay down in the straw and a few minutes later her lamb was born head first, its front feet tucked neatly under its chin. Once the head and shoulders were out the rest of the lamb's body soon slithered to the ground. Charlie, who had filmed the birth through the bars of the gate, gave them the thumbs up.

"A nice healthy ewe," said Bill with satisfaction as he cleared the mucus membranes from the lamb's mouth and head and placed her in front of her mother.

"I think we should call this one Poppy, as they share a birthday," said Scarlett.

They watched transfixed as the ewe began licking

her lamb. After a while Poppy's tiny namesake struggled to her feet, her legs wobbly as she searched for milk. Just twenty minutes after being born she was suckling contentedly.

"This little one's lucky – she has a good mum. Some of them aren't so fortunate and the ewes reject them at birth. That's why they end up as sock lambs," said Bill.

Poppy leant on the gate of the pen, thinking about mothers and daughters. Hope and Shelley. Scarlett and Pat. Isobel, Caroline. Who could tell whether or not you'd end up with a good mum, like the spindly-legged lamb in front of them? Perhaps it was all a giant lottery, down to the luck of the draw.

In which case, Poppy felt very lucky indeed.

CHAPTER 32

The date of Cloud's X-ray loomed ever closer and Poppy was counting down the days with a mixture of trepidation and excitement that gave her permanent butterflies. No matter how hard she tried not to show it, she knew Cloud sensed her tension. He radiated nervous energy and was almost bouncing off the walls of his stable after being cooped up for so long.

Finally the day arrived and once more Bill pulled up outside Riverdale with his Land Rover and trailer ready to transport Cloud to the vet centre in Tavistock. Caroline loaded Chester first and Cloud dragged Poppy up the ramp behind the donkey as if he knew it was his ticket to freedom.

"He was a nervous wreck that first time, do you remember?" said Caroline. "He's come a long way these last few months, Poppy."

"I know. It's easy to forget when you see him every

day. I think he'd still be lost without Chester though."

The vet was waiting for them in the yard. The moment Bill parked Poppy was out, undoing the bolts on the trailer. The vet watched closely as she backed Cloud slowly down the ramp and led him across the yard to the barn at the end.

"He certainly looks sound. Let's see if the proof's in the pudding, shall we?"

Poppy jiggled from one foot to the other as the vet fiddled with the X-ray equipment. Within a few minutes it was over and she was leading Cloud back to the trailer, her heart in her mouth. She followed the vet and Caroline into the consulting room where they'd first heard the news that Cloud's pedal bone was fractured and it was uncertain if he would ever fully recover.

The vet was smiling as she placed a new X-ray on a light box alongside the original.

"Well Poppy, tell me what you think," she said.

The hairline fracture that ran the length of Cloud's foot in the first X-ray had disappeared in the latest ghostly picture.

"It looks better than it was," offered Poppy, the natural born pessimist.

"I should say so. The bone has completely healed. You'd never know he'd broken it, looking at this. I'd say the box rest has done the trick. I can take the bar shoe off him today if you like," said the vet.

Poppy's heart soared. Cloud was finally, indisputably, undeniably sound. There was only one question on her lips.

"Will I be able to ride him now?"

Scarlett was waiting for them as they turned into the Riverdale drive.

"I got your text Poppy! That's fantastic news, you must be so excited. Clever Cloud. When are you going to have your first ride? Shall we go out for a hack this afternoon?" she chattered breathlessly.

"Slow down, Scarlett," laughed Caroline. "Poppy needs to take things steadily. Cloud hasn't had anyone on his back for five years, remember. I'll speak to Bella on Thursday and see what her advice is."

Privately Poppy thought there was no way she was waiting until Thursday. But she also didn't want everyone making a fuss. Since the summer she'd spent hours, days, imagining the moment she rode Cloud for the first time. But in all those daydreams it had been just the two of them. The last thing she needed was an audience. She knew everyone had her best interests at heart. But she wished they would back off.

"The first thing I'm going to do is turn him out. He's been going crazy cooped up in the stable for so long," she said firmly.

Caroline nodded her approval. "Good idea. It's so mild he won't need a rug. It'll do him good to feel the sun on his back."

Bill parked and they all piled out. Cloud whinnied and they laughed.

"He knows he's home," said Poppy. She let down the ramp of the trailer and backed him out. "I think we should put Chester in the field first, then Cloud can join him."

"How did you get on?" her dad asked, appearing from the side of the house, closely followed by Charlie and Freddie.

"As sound as a bell," grinned Poppy. "I'm just turning him out for the first time." Cloud, realising they weren't heading straight for the stables as usual, was standing stock still, his head high, sniffing the wind. Caroline undid his travel boots and unfastened his day rug and slipped it off. Poppy laid a hand on his shoulder. He trembled beneath her touch. He whinnied again and Chester answered with a deep hee haw. Poppy clicked her tongue. "Come on then. Let's go." She pulled gently on his leadrope. Cloud gave a toss of his head, his mane silver in the sun, and started dancing on the spot. Poppy could feel the pent up energy flowing through him and she tightened her hold. She clicked her tongue again and he crabbed sideways after her, through the gate and into the paddock.

"I'd better leave his headcollar on. I don't know how easy he's going to be to catch," she muttered to herself. She realised there was a side to him that she didn't know at all. This hot-headed, powerful pony who was pawing the ground in excitement was very different to the Cloud she'd spent the last few months getting to know within the safe confines of his stable.

She felt everyone watching her as she stroked his mane and unclipped the leadrope. "Stay safe," she whispered.

But Cloud didn't hear. He was off, galloping around the field, his tail high and his mane streaming. He twisted his body and gave a series of almighty bucks. Chester lifted his head to watch as he thundered past, his hooves cutting into the turf. Cloud slid to a halt in the mud by the water trough and, with a loud grunt, sank to his knees and rolled. His hooves waved wildly in the air and he rubbed his head to and fro joyfully. By the time he stood up and shook he was covered from head to toe in mud. He snorted with satisfaction and crossed the field to join Chester. Soon the pony and donkey were grazing contentedly side by side.

Bill made noises about checking his ewes and left, taking Scarlett with him. Her dad and Charlie disappeared inside to resume their game of table football, Freddie following them like a shadow. Caroline headed in the direction of her kitchen garden to dig up some leeks for dinner. But Poppy wasn't going anywhere. She sat on the post and rail fence and gazed at Cloud and Chester, her face beaming and her heart bursting with love.

CHAPTER 33

Darkness wrapped itself around the old stone cottage at the foot of the Riverdale tor like a velvet blanket. Inside Riverdale's solid stone walls the McKeevers slept deeply. All except Poppy, who had never felt more awake, more alive, in her life. Once she was sure everyone was asleep she leapt out of bed and flicked on her bedside light. The noise of the switch woke Magpie, who was curled up on the patchwork blanket at the end of her bed. He stared at her, his green eyes unimpressed.

"Sorry," she mouthed, grabbing something to wear from the untidy tangle of clothes on the floor at her feet. Within seconds she was dressed and creeping down the landing, tiptoeing to avoid the creaky floorboard outside her dad and Caroline's room. In the kitchen Freddie lifted his head and watched her pass. "I can't take you tonight Freddie, I'm sorry," she told him. He thumped his tail against the floor anyway.

Letting herself out of the back door, she saw with satisfaction that the weather forecast had been right. The low cloud cover had lifted to reveal a full moon and a sky bright with stars. She crossed the yard to the tack room and shone her torch inside. She could hear Cloud moving restlessly in the stable next door and her heart fluttered. The beam of light picked out his saddle and bridle and she scooped both up and closed the door behind her.

Cloud had been easy to catch that afternoon, after all. She'd stood at the field gate and given a low whistle and he'd cantered straight over to her.

His head appeared over the stable door now and he whickered softly. "Shh," whispered Poppy, her finger to her lips. "We mustn't wake anyone."

She'd practised tacking him up so many times over the last few weeks that she could have done it in the dark. But tonight she didn't have to. The moon cast a silvery glow over them as she fastened buckles and pulled down stirrup leathers. Cloud stood perfectly still while she worked. By the time she was ready to lead him out of the stable she felt calm and composed. His unshod hooves made only a muffled sound as she walked him to the gate that led to the moor.

Poppy knew she was taking a risk. Her natural inclination was always to play safe, to do everything by the book. Tomorrow she would. She'd listen to

Bella's advice, start slowly, take baby steps. But not tonight. Tonight was for the two of them. Poppy and Cloud. For once in her life she wanted to throw caution to the wind.

Together they stood quietly at the very edge of the moonlit moor, gazing at the Riverdale tor, Poppy's hand resting on Cloud's flank, their breathing in time. She took a deep breath, checked his girth, gathered the reins, edged a toe into the stirrup and, with a single fluid movement, swung into the saddle.

As Poppy lent down to whisper in Cloud's ear, he lifted his head, a ghost horse in the moonlight. She squeezed her legs and he danced on the spot. She laughed wildly and gave him his head. As they galloped towards the tor she crouched low over his neck, urging him faster. But Cloud needed no encouragement. The ground sped by as he stretched out his neck and lengthened his stride. Poppy felt his energy course through her. She felt elated, fearless.

But most of all, she felt complete.

ABOUT THE AUTHOR

Amanda Wills was born in Singapore and grew up in the Kent countryside surrounded by a menagerie of animals including four horses, three cats, a dog and numerous sheep, rabbits and chickens.

She worked as a journalist for more than 20 years and is now a police press officer.

Three years ago Amanda combined her love of writing with her passion for horses and began writing pony fiction. Her first novel, The Lost Pony of Riverdale, was published in 2013. The sequel, Against all Hope, followed in the summer of 2014 and the third in the series, Into the Storm, was published in January 2015.

The Riverdale Stories are currently being translated into Norwegian, Swedish and Finnish.

Find out more at www.amandawills.co.uk or like The Riverdale Stories on Facebook.

Printed in Great Britain
by Amazon.co.uk, Ltd.,
Marston Gate.